Never Cross A Boss 2

Trust Issues Book 2

Tamicka Higgins

© 2017

Disclaimer

D1444833

Chapter 1

Kayla finally decided to head back up to the hospital around 7 o'clock. She felt like that was the right time not only because evening rush hour traffic would not be an issue, but also because her mother had woken up. Kayla had to be sure to avoid really talking to her mother before she walked out the door. Luckily, her mother had been in the kitchen cooking when she finally got her clothes on. For a split second, she thought about telling her mother about the guys asking Latrell and Linell if Marcus was there. She did not know why she was thinking to do that, but there was something in her soul telling her that maybe she should say something. Going against her gut feeling, she decided not to. Marcus was not going to be there, and she wasn't going to be gone for long.

Kayla looked through the living room blinds, scanning the front of her house. In so many ways, it was eerie how she had found herself looking outside in the same way that Marcus had been earlier. Once she saw everything was good, and had figured that she was probably being way too paranoid, she pulled the door open and headed out into the already-dark evening. With no cars rolling down the street and the nearest busy street being somewhat dead, Kayla could only hear her own breathing as she crunched down the walkway between the front porch and the sidewalk. She could tell that it was starting to get really cold that night. When she breathed out of her mouth, it was very evident in the air. Plus, the side of her face stung so hard, especially at the particular moments when the wind would blow. Because Paris was such a narrow street to begin with, when the wind would blow down it, it would feel and seem a lot like a tunnel. This was especially so during the wintertime.

Kayla pulled her keys out of her coat pocket as she was making her way around the back of the car. As soon as she got inside, she immediately locked the doors. After starting the car and allowing it to warm up for a few minutes, she carefully pulled off, careful to not get stuck in a rut in the snow, and headed down to the stop sign. She rolled through and headed down to Fall Creek Place. Little did Kayla know, however, is that she was being watched at that stop sign. Soon enough, there were headlights behind her. They stayed so far back that she never even noticed them.

***

"Man," Brandon said, looking down over his boy Marcus in his hospital bed. "We gon' find the niggas that did this shit."

"Yeah," Marcus said, feeling a little hazy from being out for the surgery. "This is definitely some fucked up shit. Man, I'm just happy that Kayla didn't get hit or nothin'."

"Yeah, I feel you on that," Juan said. He then glanced through the glass of the hospital room door and into the lobby. He could feel Marcus' mama's cold eyes on him and his boy Brandon. In fact, for as long as he could remember during the time that he had been boys with Marcus, his mama had always had this look on her face when she looked at them. Juan was not the kind of dude to sweat it, though. He rarely saw the woman to begin with. "We just glad that you made it."

"Yeah, nigga," Brandon said. "When Kayla called me tellin' me what happened, I couldn't believe that shit. I was at the crib, chillin', you know, and I thought it was you callin' but it was actually her. You said you ain't see the two niggas in the black car all that well."

"I mean, I did," Marcus said. "But I can't describe'em or nothin'. It wasn't like they had blue hair or anything like that. They were just a couple of niggas. I was standing at the window, looking out and that's when they came pullin' up."

"Nigga, you betta be glad that you was watchin' your back," Brandon said. "Just think if you hadn't have been checking out the window and shit, like a real nigga do, think about how this would have ended."

"Man, I know," Marcus said, really taking a couple of moments to think about such a scenario. Ever since he had woken up after the surgery, he could feel a little tense. Slowly but surely, whatever numbing stuff the hospital had given him was going to wear off. He could only wonder how he was going to feel once that happen. Plus, on top of all that, as soon as he woke up, the doctor was there to give him even more news: he wouldn't be able to use his arm for a while and he would have to go to physical therapy. He felt lucky that he was still on his mother's health insurance. If he had not be, this really could have turned out to be a really bad situation. Nonetheless, he was happy that he made it another day. However, he could not help but to feel a little rage. The moment his eyes opened, he knew deep down that as soon as he got back to being 100 percent, he was going after whoever pulled the trigger.

The elevator door pinged in the distance. Stepping off of it was Kayla. At first, Marcus did not notice, but once he heard his mama talking, he automatically looked out into the hallway. Now more than ever, he wanted to lay up with his woman and just talk to her. He remembered the very moment that he got hit. When he fell to the ground, the last thing on his mind was Kayla. She had just gone into the bathroom, right before the car pulled up and bullets started flying into the windows. He went back to focusing on Brandon and Juan, letting Kayla chat with his mama because he knew how worried she probably would have to have been with finding out that her son was in the hospital with a bullet in the shoulder.

Kayla walked up to Lorna, kneeled down, and hugged her. She glanced at Marcus' room, seeing that Brandon and Juan were standing on either side of it and obviously engaged in conversation.

"So, what's the latest?" Kayla asked, as she was still deciding whether or not to bring up the guys in the black car that had rolled by her place. "Anything?"

Lorna looked at her son's hospital room then back to Kayla. "Well," she started. "The police came up here, or detectives or whatever. They went asking questions, you know how they always do. Marcus answered, but I don't think they got much to go on from him. It sound like he don't know who did this or why." Lorna shrugged. "I don't know. He a man now, so he gotta make his own choices. I can't make'em for him. I just wish these couple of niggas would leave. Whew, I just don't trust them."

"I was thinkin' bout what you said," Kayla said, not really sure of where she was going and how far she was going to go. "And I feel you on what you was saying about Brandon and Juan."

"Hmm, hmm," Lorna said.

"But I just don't know if I think that they did it," Kayla said. "I just don't know if I think that they were the ones that shot up Marcus' apartment."

Lorna grinned, hating that she had to be the mature person in the entire situation and have the wherewithal to give some benefit of the doubt.

"Maybe they didn't," she said, reluctantly. "But, still. They might not have been the ones to actually pull the trigger. I give them that. Maybe they did not do that part. But I bet you this...I bet you them niggas had something to do with whoever did. There are just one too many coincidences going on with them for me to not think there is some connection, if you know what I mean. I text my girlfriend earlier and asked her if she knew some more about whatever friend they used to have that got killed too, but she ain't text me back yet. I wanna know what she got to say and what she maybe know about what all happened. I wish I could remember more from the first time people told me, but shit, I forget now."

Just then, Brandon and Juan came walking down the hall. Immediately, Lorna noticed and looked up as the two of them approached the chairs.

"Well we gon' go ahead and leave now," Brandon said while Juan nodded.

"Oh, okay," Lorna said, in a voice that was clearly being forced to sound nice. "Well, y'all just make sure y'all be careful out there. And see what you hear and make sure you let me know."

"We will," Juan said.

Brandon looked at Kayla. "He saw you when you came in," he said. "You know he waitin' to see you."

Kayla looked passed Brandon and Juan. There, her eyes met with Marcus' eyes, as he was smiling at her. She smiled back as she stood up, knowing that soon enough her smile would turn into a serious tone because she needed answers to make sense of some things. Now that she knew that Juan and Brandon had been up at the hospital all of this time, she knew that they were not the two dudes that Latrell and Linell had said they'd seen when they were playing out in the snow. Still, however, Miss Lorna had a good point. Brandon and Juan may not have pulled the trigger but they may have had something to do with whoever did. What and why that could be, Kayla still did not know.

Kayla smiled and excused herself before walking down the hall. Soon enough, Brandon and Juan were stepping onto the elevator. Kayla stepped into Marcus' hospital room. Immediately, her eyes were drawn to his shoulder – to where the doctors had been operating on him. He clearly looked as if he was a little foggy from whatever they had used to put him under.

"Well, shit," Marcus said, playfully. "Ain't you gonna say wassup to a nigga or somethin? I mean, damn."

Kayla smirked a little bit then kneeled down to kiss him quickly on the lips. No matter what, she never thought of herself as the kind of chick that would kiss all up on a woman's son right in front of her.

"How you feelin?" Kayla asked.

Marcus tried to move his shoulder, not even thinking about how that is the last thing he should be doing. Immediately, he winced.

"Don't do that," Kayla said.

"I mean, a nigga alive," Marcus said then smiled. "I was more worried about you. I thought about you when I first woke up."

Kayla smiled and slid her hand into Marcus' hand. She could see in his eyes how much he loved her. There was no doubt about that. However, now she wanted to know what all was going on. Suddenly, this winter was getting very cold, very fast. Her entire walk up in the parking garage, she could not help but to look over her shoulder a couple of extra times compared to usual. She never saw anything, and tried to convince herself that she just might have been acting paranoid. Still, however, there were too many unanswered questions. As she talked to Marcus, she made sure to keep her voice down. In Kayla's mind, the jury was still out on whether or not she was going to mention the dudes coming by her house to Miss Lorna. She knew that she first wanted to talk to Marcus about it and see what he say.

Marcus picked up on Kayla's long silence. "Baby," he said. "What's wrong? I mean, I thought you'd be a little more excited than this to see me. I know my boys was here, but I asked about you first when I woke up."

"I know, Marcus," Kayla said. "I know. I'm just thinkin."

"What you thinkin' bout?" Marcus asked.

Kayla glanced back at Miss Lorna before she began explaining. "Marcus," she said. "Latrell and Linell went out to play in the snow earlier when I went home to make them something to eat."

"Yeah," Marcus said, not really sure of where this story could be going. "And?"

"And when they came in, they told me that two dudes in a black car pulled up out front of the house and asked if you were there," Kayla said. She then leaned in. "You need to tell me what is going on cause somethin' just don't feel right. Who would be shooting up your place and why? And don't try to bullshit me. I saw the way you was lookin' out of the patio door, through the blinds. It was obvious that you were keeping an eye out for somebody, so please just go ahead and tell me who. Did you tell the police?"

"What the fuck you mean did I tell the police?" Marcus asked, clearly thinking that what Kayla had just asked him was ridiculous. "Hell naw I ain't tell the fuckin' police. Why would you even ask me some shit like that?"

"Cause you sure ain't tell me," Kayla responded. "And I coulda got shot and shit, too."

Marcus grinned and looked away from Kayla. He hated how what was going on had almost affected Kayla. While he was grateful to God that she had just so happened to have walked to the bathroom right before the bullets started, he hated how everything was only dependent on a moment's time. There were so many different ways that this scenario could have gone. At the same time, he was surprised that things would come to bullets flying into his apartment building.

"Marcus?" Kayla said, grabbing his attention. "Tell me what the fuck is going on. Who are these people and why would they be coming by and asking my little brother and sister if you were there or not?"

Marcus was clearly hesitant on answering. Just as he was opening his mouth to go ahead and tell his woman what was going on, a nurse – plump, blonde white girl with blue eyes – came walking in. She smiled at Marcus.

"So, how are you feeling?" the nurse asked.

At that moment, Kayla backed away from the bed to give the nurse room to look at any machines and whatnot that she might need to tend to. She rolled her eyes, hating how just as Marcus was about to tell her, the nurse came walking in. In so many ways, the smile on her face was the exact opposite of how Kayla was feeling. Two guys coming by her house had changed this entire game.

"Oh, I'm alright," Marcus answered. "Just starting to feel a little stiff and shi—stuff, but other than that, I'm okay."

"That is certainly good to hear," the nurse said as she checked over some things on a computer screen. "Just so you know, hon, they hospital will be serving dinner in about thirty minutes or so. Doctor said you're fine to eat whatever."

"Okay," Marcus said.

"Alrighty," the nurse said, now standing in the doorway. "Just push the button if you need anything. I'll be around, okay."

"Thank you," Kayla said, smiling. She then turned back to Marcus. Marcus groaned, wishing that all of this was not happening. "Well?" Kayla said, obviously wanting Marcus to continue with this story. "What is going on, Marcus?"

"I'm not gon' explain it all to you here," Marcus said. "But it's over some work."

"Some work?" Kayla asked. "You ain't never had this problem before. What changed? Did the system change or somethin' to bein' out in them…"

"Shh," Marcus hissed, glancing out into the hallway and at his mother. She was now on the phone with someone as she sat in the waiting area. "That ain't what I'm sayin," he said. "What I'm sayin' is that these dudes that me and Brandon and Juan was dealing with…they think that I tried to fuck'em over."

"Fuck'em over?" Kayla said. "Why would they think you tried to do some shit like that, Marcus? This shit ain't makin' no damn sense to me."

"It ain't makin' as much to me, either," Marcus said. "Like I said, baby, I ain't gon tell you everything in this hospital bed like this cause you never know who might be listening. But you remember that weekend I did that trip?"

Kayla thought back for a moment. Marcus had taken a trip to and from somewhere south back right before New Year's. "Yeah, when you went down south, right?" Kayla asked.

Marcus nodded. "Yeah," he said. "Well, they basically think that on that trip, I took some of the shit off the truck. They try'na say that the right amount wasn't in there and that I got it."

Kayla's heart jumped. "Are you fuckin' serious?" she asked. "Well…Do you got they shit? If you got they shit, then just give it back."

"Hell naw I ain't got they shit," Marcus said. "What the fuck? Why the fuck would I have they shit?"

"Okay," Kayla said, realizing how that could have come across to a nigga. "My bad, my bad. But Marcus. What you…I mean, how you gon' get them to see that you ain't got they shit?"

"I'mma go talk to'em," Marcus answered.

"Talk to'em?" Kayla snapped back, shaking her head. "How you gon' go talk to the very niggas that came and put a hundred fuckin' bullets into your apartment? I don't know what you thinkin', or if it's that shit the hospital got you on, but you got shot today. It don't seem like whoever they are they are open to sitting down and havin' conversations. Hold up…Who are these dudes?"

Marcus hesitated. He really did not want to answer because he already knew how his mother felt about his boys Brandon and Juan and he was thinking that his mother might have been running her mouth as usual to Kayla. At the same time, he remembered his Uncle Charles telling him when he was growing up that he would be lucky to have one true friend in life. For Marcus, he felt twice as lucky and as if that luck might be the reason God only had this bullet hit him in the shoulder. He knew that his boys Brandon and Juan were just as confused about the situation as he was.

"They some niggas that we know," Marcus said.

"We who?" Kayla asked, wanting clarification.

"You know," Marcus said. "Me, Juan, and Brandon. Like I said, I'm not gon' tell you everything in this hospital cause I don't know who else might be coming in, but I'mma make sure all of this get taken care of."

"How you gon' do that, Marcus?" Kayla asked, not seeing how such would even be possible. "I know your doctor musta told you already that you won't be able to use your arm for a minute and that you'd have to go through physical therapy."

"Fuck," Marcus said. "I know, I know. I just don't want you to worry."

"How you gon' tell me that you don't want me to worry, Marcus?" Kayla asked. "Whoever these niggas are, they came by my place and asked my brother and sister if you was there. I think they gotta know a lot more than you think they do for them to be doing some shit like that."

Just then, Kayla felt her phone vibrate in her pocket. At first, she ignored it. However, once it continued vibrating, she finally pulled it out her pocket and looked at who was calling. It was her mother. She rolled her eyes as she shoved her phone back down into her pocket. She already knew that it was probably her mother calling about some silly shit. Right then, she was just not in the mood for it.

"Kayla," Marcus said. "I don't know what I'mma do. They think I got they shit. I don't got it and I told them like a month ago and again last week when they called me 'bout that shit that I don't have it. Whatever they gave me down in Little Rock was on that fuckin' truck. I only stopped for gas on the way back and next thing I know, I supposedly got they shit."

"How much?" Kayla asked.

"How much what?"

"How much money we talkin' with all this?"

Just as Marcus was about to explain, the hospital cafeteria worker came rolling a cart into his room. It was dinner time and he was asked to choose what specific dinner he wanted. When the nurse sat whatever he had asked for on the table in front of him, Marcus looked at it then up at Kayla.

"I'mma need some real food," Marcus said.

Within seconds, Lorna came walking up to the hospital room doorway. She smiled and waved at the cafeteria nurse as she walked by, heading down the hallway. Kayla watched as she stepped into the room.

"Marcus," she said. "I was thinkin' bout goin' to get something to eat when I saw the food people comin' round."

Everyone looked at his meal on the table. "I know that ain't gon be enough," Lorna said.

"I take whatever I can get," Marcus said.

"Aight then," Lorna said. "I'mma either go up on Martin Luther King or down on 16th Street. We'll see how I'm feelin' when I get out there. Sixteenth is closer, but I kinda want some bar-b-q."

"Thanks, Mama," Marcus said. "I don't care what it is. As long as it's better than this stuff."

Lorna looked at Kayla. "You want anything, Kayla?" she asked.

Kayla shrugged. "You don't have to," she said.

Lorna insisted on getting Kayla something to eat. Kayla went ahead and agreed and said that she would wait there until Miss Lorna got back. Soon enough, it was just Kayla and Marcus again.

"You think these dudes gon' try again?" Kayla asked.

Marcus shrugged. "I don't even know," he answered. "Probably not. I mean, they don't even know if they got me or not. I don't know how they would. There are at least two or three other cars like the car I got that be parked in the parking lot at my apartments, so I don't even know if they know if I was hope. I know my ass wasn't opening the blinds so wide that they would see me."

"Okay," Kayla said. "Then why else would they come by my place after your place done been shot up and you in the hospital cause of a bullet to the shoulder? Hold up… How they even know where the hell I live, or who I am for that matter?"

Marcus looked dead into Kayla's eyes. "Fuck if I know," he said. "You know I ain't tell'em that shit. Who the fuck knows how they know? Plus, you know how niggas be knowin' people in Indianapolis and shit. I swear, I'm ready to get the fuck up out of this place."

"Is that why you was talkin' about movin' away?" Kayla asked. "Huh? Is that why you was talkin' bout movin' down to Atlanta?"

"I had been thinkin' bout that shit anyway," Marcus said, hesitantly. "But I can't front and shit. I am gettin' tired of how small this place feel sometime."

Kayla pulled a chair up to the side of Marcus' bed and sat down. She felt her phone vibrating again. She sighed as she pulled it out of her pocket.

"Fuck," Kayla said.

"What?" Marcus asked, looking over the side of the bed.

"It's my mama," Kayla said. "She done called like three times since I fuckin' got here. She know where I am. I don't know why in the fuck she would be callin'."

"Just answer," Marcus said.

"Just answer my ass," Kayla snapped back. "You know how her ass is. I managed to get the hell out of the house when I came up here without having to talk to her ass. You know she just callin' to start some shit."

"You tell her what happen?" Marcus asked.

Kayla hesitated before answering. "Yeah," she said, nodding her head. "I told her about what happened and how you was in the hospital."

"I know she had some shit to say about that," Marcus said.

"Basically," Kayla said. Finally, her phone stopped vibrating. A MISSED CALL alert popped up as Kayla pushed her phone back into her pocket.

The room slowly got quiet between the two of them while Marcus picked over the flimsy hospital food. Thoughts kept swirling around in Kayla's head. She knew that she and

Marcus had probably talked enough about whatever went down with the two dudes that had shot up his place. Kayla prayed to God that they were just doing it to scare him, or maybe that they would think, or not even know any different, that they had maybe gotten Marcus. Whatever they thought, Kayla now wanted to know why whoever these dudes were would come by her house after the shooting. Was Miss Lorna right in thinking that Brandon and Juan had something to do with it? Kayla wanted to think not, but life had taught her enough as this point to where she knew better. She knew that sometimes the ones who were closest to you would be the first to do you dirty. Now, Kayla knew that she would just have to wait…and waiting under these circumstances was just not comfortable.

***

Rolanda dropped her cell phone onto the floor, her eyes barreling down on her nine year old twins Latrell and Linell. As the cold metal of the end of a pistol pressed against the temple of her head, she could not help but to sweat. Tears practically streamed down her face as she felt the gun nudge into her head.

"Please don't," Rolanda pleaded. "Please, don't do this."

"Call her again," the man said.

Rolanda angled her eyes up and glanced at the tall, somewhat buff dark skinned man. In the darkness of her living room, he looked ten times as scary as he did when he'd forced his way into the backdoor, then into the kitchen. Out of instinct, Rolanda was about to react. She had been frying fish and her first reaction was to throw the pan of hot grease at the nigga who had forced his way into her house. However, once her eyes lay on the end of a metallic pistol, she was practically frozen with terror. Within seconds, another man had come walking in behind this one. Like the first, he also had a gun and a look of anger in his face that was malicious. Almost like a planned operation, the guy who had come in second rushed into the living room and got Linell and Latrell together, holding them in the corner by the television and telling them to be quiet. Within minutes, Rolanda was on her knees with a gun to her head and being told to call her daughter.

"Was is this about?" Rolanda demanded to know. "Why the fuck are y'all doing this shit to me and my kid? Why? What the fuck is this about?"

Without even speaking, the man holding a gun to Rolanda's head used his free hand to slap her across the back of her head. He used all of his force and Rolanda could feel it. She was getting a little dizzy as the back of her head stung. All the while this happened, like any mother, her eyes were stuck on her kids on the other side of the room. The terrified look in their eyes was enough to break any mother's heart. They truly looked innocent and confused.

"Bitch, do what the fuck I said," the man said. "Call your daughter again. We need to know what fuckin' hospital room. Call her, shit."

Rolanda did as she was told, slowly reaching down and grabbing her cell phone. She called Kayla again, praying to God that she would answer so she could get whatever information they wanted so that these nigga could leave and stop terrorizing her and her kids.

The man holding the gun to Rolanda's head looked up and across at his accomplice, who stood over the kids in the corner. "Nigga, I know we saw her head down to that hospital," he said.

"Yeah," his guy said. "So the little niggas wasn't lyin'. That nigga wasn't here. He in the hospital."

Rolanda could feel the eyes on her as she was listening to the phone ring. Once again, rather than hearing Kayla's voice answer "hello," Rolanda was faced with yet another voicemail greeting. She cringed, hoping and praying that neither one of these crazy niggas would get the idea of blowing she or her kids' brains out.

"She ain't answer," Rolanda said, reluctantly. "I called again and she ain't answer."

"Bitch," the man said. "I know she must'a told you what room he was in."

Rolanda shook her head. "No," she said. "I swear to God she didn't tell me."

"You her mama," he said. "What kinda bitch – cause that's what she is to me, just like you – don't tell her mama what room her boyfriend in when he take a bullet? That's how I know you lyin."

"I swear," Rolanda said. "I don't know what fuckin' room he is in. And we don't talk like that no way. I saw her when she came home and she told me what happened at that he was in Methodist, but I don't know what room."

The man nudged Rolanda's head with the gun again. This time, however, he did it so hard that her head moved several inches over. No matter how long – how many minutes – Rolanda felt that cold still pressed against her head, it was just something that she could never get used to. It was as if it never stopped being cold; whenever he moved the gun, she could not help to think that he would next be moving his finger. Her entire life flashed before her eyes.

"I think this bitch lyin," the man said to his partner.

His partner nodded. "Yeah, nigga," he said, agreeing. "Somethin' about her just don't seem like she the real truthful type."

"I know what, though."

"What?"

The man chuckled, looking down at Rolanda's cowering body. "We not gon' leave dis house till we know where the fuck that nigga is," he said. "We followed her ass when she left and saw that she went right on down to the hospital, so we know that he in there."

"Man, I told you that we shoulda ran up in his shit instead of doin' the drive-by thing," the guy standing over the kids staid.

"Nigga, shut up!"

Rolanda could hear this voice boom.

"We gotta figure out what we gon' do with these motherfuckas until we get some answers."

"Please don't kill my kids," Rolanda pleaded. "Please, I'm beggin' you. Please don't kill my kids. They ain't done nothin'. They don't know shit about none of this shit. I swear they don't. Please, just don't kill my kids."

The man standing over Rolanda snickered. "Bitch, shut the fuck up," he said. "What the fuck you think we are, animals? We ain't gon kill no fuckin' kids. You just work on getting' in touch with you daughter so we can figure out what fuckin' hospital room that nigga is in. The sooner you find that out for us, the better off you and your kids gon' be. The kids' cell phones? Where are they? You think she would answer one of them instead of you?"

Rolanda shook her head. "I don't know," she answered. "I don't know where their phones are and I don't know if she would answer them or not. I don't even know if she lookin' at her phone. I swear to fuckin' God, I don't know."

Latrell and Linell struggled with which man scared them more. The one standing over them definitely was not as aggressive as the guy standing over their mother. However, he was much closer. Linell's eyes swelled up with tears, not only scared for herself but also scared for her mother. She and Latrell had been sitting in the living room when there was a knock at the door. Their mama had seen a silhouette of a man, through the curtains, standing on the front porch. At first, she had assumed that it was her friend, Kevin, stopping by. Linell remembered watching her mother practically walk toward the door with a smile on her face. Just when she got to it and opened it to a face she did not know, the back door was being pushed in. Guns were pointed at them. Suddenly, the television became light background noise.

Latrell, on the other hand, was not quite as emotional as his sister. With how he was sitting, pushed back into the corner with part of his body out of sight because of the couch and the shadow that it cast over him, he started to pull his phone out of his pocket. The man standing over them seemed so close, but Latrell knew that he had to try something. He figured he would try to call Daddy. Being careful to not move his head too much, he glanced down ever so slightly as he scrolled through the contacts on his phone. At first, he had passed Daddy, then had to go back. He hoped to God that the dude standing over him and his sister with a gun would not notice. Latrell tried to keep his phone as pushed into the dark corner as he could– between the back of the couch and the wall.

"Ay nigga," the man standing over Rolanda said. "Get one of them little niggas' phones and have'em call they sister. We gon' find out where this nigga is and shit. Oh yeah, we gon' find him."

Just then, Latrell could feel a shadow coming over his body. His heart jumped as he looked up and found that he had been caught trying to use his phone.

"What the fuck you doin' lil' nigga?" the man said, leaning over and snatching Latrell's phone up off of the floor quickly. "Look, nigga," he was now saying to his buddy standing over the mother. "This nigga was over here on his phone already."

"He ain't call the police did he?"

The man looked through Latrell's call log then shook his head. "Naw, he ain't call nobody," he said. "Let's see if we can find this sister number, though. Hold up." He scrolled through Latrell's contacts until he got down to Kayla. He called, holding the phone up to the side of his face. Just as what had happened with Rolanda, it went straight to voicemail. Looking at his partner, he shook his head. "She ain't answer."

"Who was you callin' lil' nigga?" the man standing over Rolanda asked.

Latrell, who was nervous, looked across and up into the eyes of the man standing over his mother. It was so hard for him to pull his eyes away from his pleading mother, on her knees with a gun to her head. Quickly, he shook his head. "Nobody," he said. "I was just lookin' for my sister number like you was saying."

The man nodded, pressing the gun harder into Rolanda's head. Rolanda shook uncontrollably as she felt the metal push into the side of her head. More than anything at that very moment, she wanted to lunge across the room and crouch down over her children. However, she knew that if she made any quick move like that, there would surely be a gun going off on either side of the room.

"Well," the man said. "Look like we just gon' have to wait now, don't it. She gotta come home eventually. And I ain't leavin' till I find out where this nigga is."

"Why the fuck are you doin' this?" Rolanda asked. "Huh? Why the fuck you doin' this to me and my kids?"

The man snickered. "Boo, shut the fuck up," he said. "There's been, let's say a little snag in things, and this is how we gon' work it out. Now, shut the fuck up with all that cryin' before we really give you somethin' to cry about."

***

Myesha grabbed her bag and walked through her parents' polished white room, which was the living room of the house. She double checked herself, making sure that she had grabbed everything she was supposed to grab. Ever since she had gotten off the phone with her best friend Kayla earlier, there was a sense of worry that had come over her. Often, when she found herself thinking about everything Kayla had told her, she would also find her head shaking. The situation Kayla was in could have been way different. Myesha's eyes almost swelled with tears at the very thoughts of Kayla getting hit with one of the bullets that came flying into Marcus' apartment. She just thanked God that Kayla was in the bathroom, meaning she had several walls between the shots and herself. Those walls were probably what saved her.

As soon as Myesha had gotten off the phone with Kayla, she told her mother what happened. In her usual sense, she went on and on about Myesha needing to watch out in case any of the backlash just so happened to come her way when she was hanging out with Kayla. Myesha shrugged that entire thing off, knowing in the back of her mind that Kayla could very well be involved in some really deep shit and not even know it. She could only hope that her girl would play her cards smart, and maybe even stay as far away from Marcus as possible for a while. There was no doubt in Myesha's mind that whoever shot up Marcus' apartment like that was trying to kill him, not just scare him. And once the word got around to whoever these dudes are that Marcus got hit but was not killed, they would surely come back and try again. Niggas around here just had too much time on their hands not to, in Myesha's eyes.

Myesha was now on her way to meet up with one of her classmates. She and a classmate were sharing a book for their literature class. The classmate had made copies of certain chapters and was now ready to trade the book off to Myesha so she could use it. Myesha pulled the front door open and pushed herself out into the wind.

"God, I hate this snow," she said to herself. The wind was moving strong enough now that it picked up snow in its path and blew it into Myesha's face.

Myesha walked down the sidewalk between the front porch and the sidewalk and started her car. Already, from when she'd gotten home earlier, she could see that she would need to brush some of the snow off of her car. While her car warmed up, she grabbed her scraper out of the backseat. One end was the actual scraper while the other end was a large brush. As she brushed the snow off of her windshield then back window, she still could not help but to think about Kayla. Over and over again, she just hoped that she watched her back. The last thing she ever wanted to do was to turn on the news and see that her best friend had been killed. That would just break her heart into a thousand little pieces.

While Myesha was brushing the snow off of her car and allowing it to warm up some, she also decided that she would hit her girl Kayla up later on. She could tell when she was talking on the phone with her earlier that her stress was probably through the roof. And rightfully so, Myesha thought. In fact, she was already trying to think of ways to help Kayla's mind stay off of what was going on. She'd almost lost her man. Myesha had had a couple of boyfriends during high school and after, but she'd never been lucky enough to have anything as serious as what Kayla had with Marcus. Rather, Myesha let it go and put it into God's hands to send her a man when he was ready for her to have one.

Once Myesha got her front and back windows wiped off, she quickly climbed into the driver's seat of her car and slammed the door. She shook, immediately reaching down and turning on the heat.

"Whew, it's cold," she said to herself.

Myesha flipped on the radio, turning to Hot 96.3, then slowly pulled out of the parking spot. As she slowly rolled down the street, making her way over to the main street so she could head over to Indiana Avenue – close to IUPUI – she drove passed Kayla's house. The house was completely dark except for a faint light on the first floor. After noticing that, Myesha noticed that a car she'd never seen was parked out front. Immediately, she thought of Kayla's mother, Rolanda. Myesha liked to think that she liked everyone, but there was just something about her best friend's mother that just did not sit well with her. After all, Myesha had known Kayla for almost as long as she could remember – from when her mama and daddy were married to the divorce to her mother basically having a midlife crisis of sorts.

Myesha shook her head as she focused on the road in front of her, assuming that Kayla's mother probably had some man over again. There were nights, especially when little Latrell and Linell were spending time with their daddy for the weekend, where Kayla would text Myesha and tell her that her mother had some man over. There was even a night where Kayla was scared half to death when she came out of her bedroom and practically walked dead into a tall, somewhat buff darker skinned man who was easily old enough to be her father. Kayla had told Myesha how the man was dressed in just boxers – boxers that did little to actually conceal his manhood. Myesha could only shake her head at the thought of her careless and reckless her girl Kayla's mother was becoming. There was no doubt in her mind that she would use this time – time when Kayla is sitting at the hospital because her boo had been shot – to have some man over and not have to worry about Kayla's scolding looks.

Myesha could only imagine what Kayla was going through. She just kept her eyes on the snowy road as she headed over to IUPUI. She knew that as soon as she traded this book with her classmate, she was going to hit her girl up and let her know that she was there for her.

Chapter 2

"Man, this shit is fucked up," Brandon said.

After Brandon and Juan left their boy Marcus' hospital room, they walked downstairs to the parking garage. For the first several minutes of the journey, neither of them said a word to the other. Once they got out into the parking garage, starting to walk a little fast so they could hurry up and get out of the cold wind, the tension was getting to be too much for even two dudes to completely ignore.

"I know, man," Juan said. "This shit is some fucked up stuff. I mean, who you think did this?"

Brandon shrugged. "A lot of this shit just don't make no sense to me."

The two of them climbed into Brandon's Chevy Impala. Quickly, Brandon turned the engine over and started blaring the heat so it could warm up.

"Whoever the fuck did this shit, we need to find'em," Juan said, getting comfortable into his seat. "You already know what gon' happen."

"What you mean?" Brandon asked. "What's gon happen?"

Juan looked at his boy Brandon with this face that told him that he should definitely already know what was going to happen. "Nigga, is you serious?" he said. "You know how this shit gon' play out. Whoever the fuck did shot Marcus' place up was prolly try'na kill his ass."

Brandon looked away. "Nigga, they coulda just been scaring him or something," he said, not trying to hear that.

"Nigga," Juan said. "You know how these niggas out here is. They will kill you over a pair of fuckin' shoes. And think about this – whoever was firing them shots into his apartment like that, if they was just trying to scare him, you already know that they would have jus fired like a couple shots into his apartment. Not no damn full round, or so it sounded like based on what Marcus was sayin'. Dude...I don't know what the fuck you thinkin', but I think this shit was a hit."

Brandon shook his head. "Naw," he said. "A hit? A hit over what, nigga?"

"Whatever the fuck happened with Marcus and that work when he went down south," Juan said. "You already know we wasn't gon' talk about that shit a lot in the hospital room like that. But you know that is exactly what the fuck was goin' through his mind. How was it not goin' through yours?"

"Yeah, but..." Brandon said, his words trailing off.

"Nigga, I'm tellin you," Juan said. "Whoever the fuck did this shit is gon' try again once they find out that Marcus didn't get killed. I would fuckin' bet that shit on my life, nigga. Whoever shot that many damn bullets into his apartment was try'na kill his ass. And they gon' try again once they find out that they didn't do it this time. Why wouldn't they?"

Brandon reversed out of the parking lot and headed toward the parking garage exit. "So, what you sayin?" he asked.

"Nigga, I'm sayin' that we gotta find out who the fuck this is before they try again," Juan said. "Think about it. Marcus ain't gon' be able to do shit. You already heard what they said up in his room about his arm and needing physical therapy and all that until he'll be able to use his arm again. His shoulder is pretty fucked up. Think about it, he ain't even gon' be able to drive. So, what do you think that mean for him?"

Brandon nodded, knowing where this was going.

"Exactly," Juan said, turning and looked ahead. "Our boy is gon' be just a fuckin' sittin' duck for real, until whoever these niggas are find out that they didn't get him and then find out where the fuck he is. You can bet that on everything, nigga. They gon' definitely try again."

Just then, Brandon thought about it all. He looked over at his boy. "Terrell," he said.

"Terrell?" Juan said, trying to figure out what Brandon was talking about.

"Yeah, Terrell," Brandon said. "How much you wanna bet that he know some shit about all of this?"

Juan nodded as he thought about it. "Or," he said. "Maybe he know somebody that do. He the one who got

Marcus in touch with what's his name up here – the nigga who got him interested in making that trip."

"That nigga Hakim," Brandon said.

Just then, Brandon pulled the car up to the parking garage exit. He paid the attendant, quickly glancing over the edge of the window to have a look at her body. Her face was not all that, but he could definitely see that she had a shape. Nice chest; flat stomach – he just had to see what the ass look like. He smiled as he pulled off and headed out toward Capital Street. When he came up to the stop sign, he stopped and looked at his boy.

"You think Hakim coulda had something to do with this shit?" Brandon asked.

Juan shrugged. "Shit, I mean…" he said. "Maybe. We don't even know what the fuck went wrong, if anything went wrong."

"I bet that nigga Terrell do, though," Brandon said.

Juan nodded. "It's gotta either be one of them niggas," he said.

"Bet," Brandon said, pulling his phone out of his pocket. "I'mma hit this nigga up right now."

"What?" Juan said. "You try'na go see him or something?"

"Nigga, like you said," Brandon said. "We gotta handle this shit before it get even worse. We can't just let our boy get killed out here like that if we know that we coulda did something to stop it. That ain't what real niggas do. I'm seein' what you said, nigga."

"Yeah," Juan said. "I'm tellin' you. Whoever this is, they gon' try again. I wonder what coulda went that wrong, though, to where Hakim, if it is Hakim, woulda put a fuckin' hit out on Marcus's life like that."

"Wait up, wait up," Brandon said. The phone was ringing.

After several rings, Terrell picked up. Music played in the background; his voice was very groggy to say the least. "Yea?" he answered.

"Wassup, nigga?" Brandon said. "This Brandon."

"Aww, wassup B?" Terrell said.

"Shit," Brandon said. "Ay, man, you hear about our boy Marcus?"

"Naw, what happened?" Terrell asked.

Brandon glanced at Juan then focused back on the phone call. "Nigga, somebody shot up his place earlier today."

"Word?" Terrell asked. "Is you fuckin' serious?"

"Yea," Brandon said. "I'm with Juan right now. We actually just leaving the hospital. I was try'na see if we could come through real quick and holla at you and shit. I can tell you the rest when we get over there."

Terrell groaned, clearly not feeling like company at the moment. However, with something this serious, he already knew how it would look if he made himself unavailable.

"Come thru," Terrell told Brandon. "I got a chick over here, so I don't usually let otha niggas come over when I'm chillin' like that and shit, but for this occasion, shit I will. Come thru."

"Aight then," Brandon said, then hung up the phone.

Brandon turned the car onto Capital and headed toward Haughville. "We gon' figure out who did this shit," he said. "Ain't no niggas about to take out my boy like that if I can help it."

"We goin' over to Terrell's?" Juan asked.

Brandon nodded. "Yeah?"

"You got that heat on you, don't you?" Juan asked, referring to the Brandon's gun.

Brandon nodded. "Nigga, you know I stay with that shit," he said. "It's too dangerous out here to not be. For all we fuckin' know, whoever this is that shot up Marcus' place and basically tried to kill him, could come after us next or some shit. You just never fuckin' know."

Juan shook his head. "Yeah," he said. "You right about that. And you know what they say: better you than me."

***

Terrell was an older dude, in his early thirties, who was known for staying in the strip club every weekend. Not only was he popular and pretty well liked with everyone that he knew, this dude was also known for having all the chicks. It was not uncommon for niggas to have to wait outside, in their cars or standing on the curb, for Terrell to get done handling his business. He lived in a little house on King Street, one of the roughest streets in a neighborhood on the near west side of Indianapolis called Haughville. Some of the hardest niggas in the city lived over here, and it had always been that way.

Brandon turned down the narrow street, looking closely for a house on his right with a red brick porch and white siding to let him know that he was there. Once he saw the house, he pulled into a spot not too far down from Terrell's walkway and called.

"Wassup?" Terrell answered. "You outside?"

"Yeah," Brandon said.

"Aight," Terrell said. "Come on up."

Brandon hung up the phone took of his seatbelt.

"Dude, I think he got some hoe over," Brandon said.

Juan chuckled. "So," he said, sarcastically. "That don't do me to good."

"I know, man," Brandon said. "He be havin' some hoes over there that I wouldn't mind smashin' my damn self."

"I ain't touchin' them," Juan said. "You already know that Terrell will fuck your ass up if you fuck around with his."

"Nigga, what you mean?" Brandon said. "Hell yeah, I know. I just look and do not touch. Best believe that ain't no problem I want to have. I can only imagine what the fuck that nigga do over some shit like that."

Brandon and Juan climbed out of Brandon's Chevy Impala, headed across the street, and up Terrell's walkway. Moments after Brandon knocked on the screen door, the front door open. A chick unlocked the screen door. "Come on in," she said, grabbing her chest. "It's cold as fuck out there."

Brandon and Juan hurried inside and closed the door behind them. There, in Terrell's dimly lit front room, they watched as a bad redbone, naked as the day she was born, hurried back to Terrell's bedroom.

"Just gimme a minute, aight?" Terrell announced from his room. The redbone hurried into his bedroom and shut the door while Brandon and Juan sat down on the sectional.

For the next several minutes, the sounds of slurping and slobbering seeped through the walls.

"Damn," Brandon said quietly, smiling. "That bitch got that throat."

"Sure sound like it, don't it?" Juan said, snickering.

The two of them sat there while they could hear the redbone who had opened the door sucking Terrell's dick from his bedroom, which was next to the living room. Soon enough, Terrell was groaning and saying that he was about to cum. Once he did, he could be heard telling the chick to "swallow Daddy's nutt."

Brandon chuckled at Juan as they both shook their heads. It was crazy to the both of them how Terrell only kept the baddest of the bad around him. And he could get them to do anything that he wanted. That was how they knew that that nigga had money. Bitches flocked to him and would come practically limping out of his bedroom. Brandon and Juan waited to see the same chick come out of Terrell's bedroom. Instead, the door swung open and Terrell stepped out into the short bedroom hallway, pulling his pants up to his waist. He stepped into the living room.

"Wassup?" he said, shaking Brandon's hand then Juan. "Had to handle some business real quick, get this nut off."

"You cool, nigga," Juan said.

"Yeah, nigga," Brandon said. "We ain't trippin?"

"Y'all wanna smoke?" Terrell asked.

Brandon and Juan would normally jump at the chance to smoke, especially with Terrell. Terrell only ever had the best of the best smoke. However, today was a little different. Neither of them were there just for social purposes. Front and center at both of their minds was finding out who could be trying to kill their boy. Respectfully, they both declined. Terrell nodded, understanding and being able to see in their face that today was just one of them days. He plopped down into a seat at the other end of the couch.

"So Marcus' place got shot up?" Terrell asked. "When that shit happened?"

"Man," Brandon said. "Like earlier today, maybe in the middle of the day or some shit."

"Damn," Terrell said. "In the middle of the fuckin' day."

Juan nodded. "Yeah," he said. "We just now comin' from the hospital and shit."

"Word?" Terrell said. "Sorry to hear that. Where that nigga get hit?"

"In his shoulder," Brandon answered. "Lost a lot of blood and shit. His girl was over when it all happened, but she ain't get hit, luckily. She pretty shook up over it."

"Bet she is," Terrell said. "That's the way that shit be, though. That's part of the reason it's hard for a real nigga to find a real chick."

"I feel you on that," Brandon said. "So, anyway, that's why we decided to hit you up. We try'na figure out who the fuck did this shit. Who the fuck would try to take out Marcus like that? Who the fuck would do some shit like this?"

Terrell looked into both Juan and Brandon's eyes, then away. He grabbed a pack of cigarettes off of a small table at the other end of the couch and lit one.

"I guess y'all don't know, huh?" Terrell said.

Immediately, Brandon and Juan's attention was peaked. They looked at each other then at Terrell.

"We don't know what?" Brandon asked.

Terrell was clearly being hesitant. From busting his nut just minutes ago, his body was relaxing while his mind caught back up to the rest of the world. Right now was probably one of the worst times for Brandon and Juan to be coming through. Jalice, the thick redbone in the other room, was incredibly busy sometimes and he really didn't get a lot of time to spend with her and that deep throat she had. Nonetheless, he knew that what he was going to say needed to be said.

"Y'all boy Marcus is in some deep shit out here," Terrell said. "I'm surprised that he ain't tell y'all niggas if he supposed to be your boy like that."

"Man," Brandon said. "He was try'na talk to us and shit at the hospital, but you know how that be. People coming and going. Plus, the fuckin' police came up to see him and shit, you we definitely was gon' try to be outta sight when they came walkin' through the door."

"No doubt," Terrell said. "That's prolly for the best. Your boy is in some deep shit over two things really, but both over that trip he made down south for Hakim."

Brandon looked at his boy Juan. Much like any two people in a long lasting friendship, one could tell what the other was thinking just by looking into their eyes.

"So, what?" Juan asked, wanting to know. "What the fuck happened? Why the fuck would Hakim be after him? He drove down and got the shit and brought it back up just like he was asked to do."

"Yes and no," Terrell said. "Last I heard, they lookin' for his ass because some of the shit was missing."

"Missing?" Brandon asked, clearly surprised. "What the fuck you mean some of the shit was missing?"

"Fuckin' missin', nigga," Terrell said. "Like he was supposed to go and bring back a certain amount but that amount wasn't there when Hakim got the car."

"And now Hakim think that our nigga Marcus stole his shit on the ride back?" Brandon asked.

Terrell nodded, slowly, as he took another hit of his cigarette. "That's what they say," he said.

"That's fuckin' bullshit," Juan said. "Why the fuck would Marcus take some of Hakim' shit like that? He know damn well that Hakim ain't the kind of the nigga you prolly fuck with like that. He know that if he do some shit like that, then yeah, somebody gon' be after his ass."

"That was the same thing I was wondering," Terrell said. "But that ain't all the hot water your boy in."

Brandon looked at Terrell, almost in disbelief at what he had just been told. It was hard enough to believe that, let alone to think that there could be more. After a couple moments of silence, Terrell told them.

"Hakim also after that nigga over some chick," Terrell said.

"Some chick?" Brandon asked.

"Yep," Terrell said, nodding. "Apparently your boy dipped in some pussy he wasn't supposed to be in and now that shit gon' catch up with him."

"Who?" Juan asked.

Terrell shook his head. "Hakim's chick," he answered. "Tweety."

***

Time seemed to go so slow but so fast while Kayla was up at the hospital with Marcus. Before either of them knew it, his mama Lorna had come back with food. The three of them sat in Marcus' hospital room, eating fried rice for a Chinese restaurant down the street. Still, there were so many unanswered questions on Kayla's mind. Sure, she wanted more than anything for Marcus to get back. However, she wanted to hurry up and get to a place where she felt like she could really talk to Marcus without them having to sorry about somebody listening. There was still so much to this story that was not making any sense – so many gaps that could not be overlooked.

Kayla had ignored her phone vibrating again. For the second time, she looked and saw that it was her mother calling. That was all she needed to know to not answer. Anytime her mother was calling back to back like that, it meant that she would want Kayla to come home so she could go lay up with some nigga somewhere. There was no doubt about it in Kayla's mind. And she was not about to let her mother take her precious time with Marcus away from her, especially not with what all was now going on. She would go home whenever she felt like it and her mother would just have to actually be that – a mother – until that time came.

When they were halfway done eating their shrimp fried rice, the doctor came walking back into Marcus' hospital room.

"I'd say you were pretty lucky," the doctor said. "This could have been a lot worse."

Lorna, letting her son be a man, simply sat over in the corner and did not say a word.

"I know," Marcus said. "I know."

"But I've got good news for you now, Marcus," the doctor said and smiled. "At first, which is usual with a gunshot victim, the plan was to keep you overnight. However, with the construction going on at the other location, this location specifically is getting a lot of the overflow. Therefore, hospital administration is pushing us to let patients go home who really do not need immediate care. And you would be one of those patients today."

Marcus smiled and let out a deep breath. Those were just the words he needed to hear. Hospitals already were not his favorite kind of place to be, let alone actually spending the night in one. For him, it wasn't even the whole people-die-in-hospitals things. Rather, it was how cold they were and how he could never really get relaxed.

"The surgery is done and went just fine," the doctor said. "I think the glass, which I read was your patio door, if I'm not mistaken?"

Marcus nodded. "Yeah," he said. "My patio door."

"Well, if my memory serves me correctly, with how patio doors are made in residential units nowadays, I'd say it was thick enough to take a lot of the impact off of the bullet off of you," the doctor said. "That's why during the operation, the bullet didn't get all that deep into your shoulder. However, that doesn't mean that you won't need some physical rehabilitation. Where the bullet struck was more-so a problem than its actual force. However, if you feel fine, I can let you go home tonight. You will have to make an appointment to see me within a week, however. No exceptions."

"I understand," Marcus said.

The doctor smiled at Marcus, then he turned to Lorna and Kayla and smiled at them. "Alright, Marcus," he said. "I will talk to the nurse about how soon we can get you wrapped up and get you outta here. It make take a little while with what else is going on in the hospital tonight. However, I will see what she says and will come back and let you know."

"Thank you, Doctor," Lorna said.

As the doctor backed out of the room and walked away, Lorna sat her food down on a table next to her and approached her son's bed.

"So, what you gon' do?" Lorna asked.

"What you mean?" Marcus said. "What I'mma do about what?"

"I mean, I guess you gon' have to come stay with me, Marcus," Lorna said. "From what it sound like, you can't go back to your apartment so I hope you wasn't thinking that that was going to happen. You gon' have to make sure that you talk to your landlord tomorrow or something and figure out what is going to go on over there with that."

"I know," Marcus said.

There was a long pause. At first, Lorna wasn't going to bring it up in from of her son's girlfriend. However, she had been thinking about how much she liked Kayla and was really getting to know her. She glanced at Kayla then back at her son.

"So, Marcus," Lorna said. "Who do you think you got after you?"

Lorna already had her own theories on things, but she wanted to hear what Marcus would have to say – to hear his explanation.

"Mama, I don't know," Marcus said. "I ain't think I had nobody after me."

"Well, somebody is, Marcus," Lorna said. "They shot up your apartment and almost killed you. Have you thought about if they come back?"

Marcus looked away from his mother, at the hospital window. It looked out at the dark, cold skyline of downtown with cars on the interstate coming around a bend. When he looked back at his mother, his eyes were met with stern, motherly eyes. He knew that she was waiting on an answer and was probably not going to just let the conversation die like he wanted.

"Marcus?" Lorna asked, not liking that her son was ignoring her. "Do whoever these people you don' got mixed up with know where I live?"

Immediately, Marcus started shaking his head. "I don't even know why you try'na talk about this," he said. "Naw they don't know where you live. That's why they came and only shot up my place."

"You know they gon' try again," Lorna said. "We gon' have to do something with you?"

"Do something with me?" Marcus asked. "What the hell you talkin' bout, Mama?"

Lorna tapped Marcus' wrist and tightened her lips. "Watch your mouth," she warned. "And what I'm sayin' is that you prolly gon' really have to lay low or something until…"

"Until what?" Marcus asked, clearly in his feelings.

"Until the police or whoever figure out what the fuck is going on," Lorna said. "Until maybe you ain't gotta worry about whoever this is coming after you and trying to blow your fuckin' head off. Think about it, son."

"I ain't gon let somebody just run me up out of the city like that," Marcus said.

Immediately, Lorna's head started shaking. She backed away from her son's bed. "I swear," she said softly to herself before raising her voice just a little. "Marcus, I told you where that life you chose leads to. I know I specifically remember telling you that shit and you did not want to listen. I told you to carry your ass on downtown and get enrolled in school or something and instead you chose to hang out with them no good niggas you call friends. And now look what done happen."

"Mama," Marcus said. "You ain't try'na say that you think that Brandon and Juan had somethin' to do with this, do you?"

Lorna snapped her neck. "Yep," she said, confidently. "You already know that that is exactly what I am trying to say. You know how I feel about them couple of friends of yours. Something about them just don't seem right."

Listening to Miss Lorna go on about her distrust of Marcus' friends, Brandon and Juan, Kayla wanted to stand up so bad and say something. She was not necessarily all that fond of Brandon and Juan, either. However, after finding out earlier that a car rolled by her place and asked Latrell and Linell if Marcus was there, told her that the people looking for Marcus could not have been Brandon and Juan. Kayla knew this because of when she had gotten back up to the hospital in the evening and learned that Brandon and Juan had yet to leave in all that time.

"Mama," Marcus said, getting angry. "You trippin'. I know my boys. It was not them, so ain't no point in us even talkin' bout this. I know it wasn't them."

"And how is that, Marcus?" Lorna asked. "Huh? How is that that you would just oh so surely know that it wasn't them who did this shit to you? According to what you said, and to what Kayla said, it was just the two of you at your apartment when it got shot up. They wasn't there, right?"

"Right," Marcus said, really having to bite his tongue from saying more. He was well aware that his mother had never really cared for Brandon or Juan. To Marcus, she found that to be so sad considering that Brandon and Juan had practically been like brothers to him – like the brothers that he never had.

"So, it could be them," Lorna said. "Don't argue with me. I'm tellin' you. Sometimes, the people that you think are your friends, ain't really your friends. And if you insist on living in that life – the life we not gon talk about – then you really gotta know that some of these niggas out here ain't really on your side. I think you need to do what is best for you."

"I'm a grown man," Marcus said.

"You almost died today, son," Lorna said. "And you are still my child no matter how grown you get. I almost died my damn self crying on the way over here from work when Kayla called me and told me what happened. You wanna know what I really think?"

"What?" Marcus asked, knowing that his mother was about to tell him whether he wanted to know or not.

"I think you should go stay with your cousin Larry up in Fort Wayne," Lorna said. "It would put you out of dodge for a while in case these people try to come back and try again once they hear that not one of their bullets killed you. And trust me, I really do think that they gon' come back and try again. This wasn't no fuckin' warning or no shit to scare you, Marcus. This was a hit no matter how you look at it. And once they find out that you alive and well and walking around, they gon' try again. I bet they will."

Just as Lorna was finishing her sentence, she could feel a dark presence coming over her. She turned toward the doorway to find her brother, Roy, approaching the doorway. Roy could only be described as tall and burly. His beard was particularly thick, especially during the winter months. A black hat sat on his bald head. At six foot five inches tall, the 42 year old had a presence about him that just sort of commanded the attention and respect of the room. Dressed in a black suede coat, black jeans, and a red button-up shirt, he stepped into the room. Immediately, Lorna rolled her eyes.

"Hey, wassup Roy?" Lorna said, greeting her brother.

Roy gave Lorna a quick hug and could instantly feel how cold she was. He was not going to question it though, considering that her child was laying up in a hospital bed with a gunshot wound to the shoulder at 20-something years old.

"Hello Lorna," Roy said. He then looked at Marcus. "Brandon called me earlier and told me what happened. I was on the road at the time, but I got here as soon as I could."

"Wassup Uncle?" Marcus said. A little smile formed on his face.

Lorna went and sat back down next to Kayla. The two looked at one another with Lorna rolling her eyes before she folded her eyes and legs. She clearly smelled bullshit all over her brother's showing up.

"Wassup lil' nigga," Roy said. "So, now it's time for you to tell me. What the fuck happened?"

Marcus looked at Kayla then back to his uncle.

"Me and Kayla was at my place when these two dudes pulled up and just started shooting at the apartment," Marcus said. "I was standing in front of the patio door and just so happened to be looking out when I saw'em pull up. Next thing I know, they getting out, each one holding a gun. A tried to get down as quick as a good, but...guess I couldn't get down fast enough." He pointed at his shoulder. "I got hit, in the shoulder. Earlier, the doctors operated and pulled the bullet out. Not too long ago, though, they came in here saying that I'd be able to go home tonight."

"Oh," Roy said. "Yeah?"

"Yeah," Marcus said, nodding. "They came in here talking about the hospital being crowded or some stuff and not really wanting to keep people that didn't need to be kept. The bullet didn't get that deep into me so I can go home tonight," he said.

"I know you happy to hear that," Roy said. Just then, out of the corner of his eye, he noticed Kayla sitting over next to Lorna. He smiled. "It's a good thing you weren't hurt, Kayla."

Kayla shook her head. "Naw," she said. "I wasn't. I was in the bathroom when the bullets start flying. I was washing my hands and next thing I know, it was so loud and I could hear glass breaking. I just hurried up and got down onto the floor, as low as I could."

"I see," Roy said. He stepped over to Kayla and gave her a quick hug. "Well, I am certainly glad to hear that it wasn't any worse. It really could have been."

"That's exactly what I'm saying," Lorna said. She unfolded her legs and arms then stood up and approached Marcus' bed. "That why I was just saying he need to get outta dodge until shit cool down a lil' bit. I was thinkin' he go stay with Larry, up in Fort Wayne."

"Go stay up in Fort Wayne?" Roy asked, surprised. "Why would you want him to do something like that?"

"Cause, Roy," Lorna said in a very stern way. "Whoever did this was obviously try'na take his life. And I know...I know, I know, I know...that they just gon' try again. C'mon, Roy. Help me talk some sense into this boy. You know how these niggas out here are nowadays. They ain't got shit else to do but to kill and shit. Why else would they shoot up in his apartment in broad daylight, and in a bunch of snow at that? Whoever mad at him ain't gon stop at one try, especially when they find out that the bullet didn't kill him."

Roy slowly turned back to his nephew Marcus. There were so many things that he wanted to say right then. However, he knew that they were things he could only talk with Marcus about when his mother was not around. It was already bad enough that his mother blamed him, in many ways, for getting her son involved in that life. Now, with him being shot in the shoulder, Roy knew that his younger sister would hold this over his head for as long as either of them lived.

"I don't know, Marcus," Roy said. "Your mother might be on to something. They prolly will try again. And if you go stay up in Fort Wayne for a little while, that could help. At least there would be some distance between you and these niggas."

Marcus shook his head. "That gon' make it look like I'm runnin," he said, surprised that a nigga as hard as his uncle would even be going along with such a scenario.

"Well," Roy said. "How would it have looked if that bullet had hit just a few more inches over? Then what would you be saying?"

Marcus had no choice but to be quiet. He knew what that meant and he understood exactly what his uncle was saying.

"It's the only thing that make sense to me," Lorna said. "I already talked to Larry earlier. I was talkin' to his mother and got his number from her. At least he'd be somewhere that whoever wouldn't be looking for him."

"Yeah," Roy said. "That's one way to think about it. But for how long?"

Lorna shrugged. "Fuck if I know," she said. "I'm not the one caught up in that lifestyle." Her head shook. "I told him about this stuff and now this done happened. Whatever you did, Marcus, you need to fix it."

"Who said I even did something, Mama?" Marcus asked. "Huh? Why you even gotta go there?"

"Marcus," Lorna said. "Whether you did something or not, you got some niggas after you that are trying to blow your fuckin' head off. You can act all tough and shit if you want to, but you obviously ain't tough enough to stand up to no bullet. Son, I just wish that you would use your head and shit. Stop thinking about what them so called friends of yours think. Plus, if you go up to Ft. Wayne, I don't suggest you tellin' them that you up there either."

"Who you talkin' bout, Lorna?" Roy asked.

Lorna rolled her eyes. "That Brandon and Juan," she answered. "You know I done told you how I felt about the both of them. They just look like a couple niggas that you can't trust. I don't even know why you gotta full around with those people. I swear I think they....nothing."

"You think they what?" Roy asked, wanting to hear his sister finish her sentence.

"Roy, I think they had something to do with this shit," Lorna said. "Something about them. I swear to God I think they had something to do with this shit. There are just too many coincidences for me, on top of them both being some shady little fucks."

"Lorna," Roy said. "I think you need to calm down and think about what'chu saying. Why would Brandon and Juan do this to they boy Marcus?"

"Why wouldn't they?" Lorna asked. "Roy, you wasn't born yesterday and you certainly not new out on them streets. You know how niggas get jealous and stuff, for whatever reason. I don' t know and I don't want to know. I was just lettin' it be known how I feel about all this."

At this point, Kayla could not take anymore. She knew now more than ever that she needed to let them all know what she knew. If nothing else, it would put Lorna's mind at ease so she would not have to blame Brandon and Juan anymore. Kayla stood up and approached the bed.

"Well, actually," Kayla said, hesitantly. "At first, I wasn't gon say nothin' Miss Lorna, because I kinda thought the same thing, but..."

"But what, Kayla?" Lorna asked, clearly very concerned and interested. "But what?"

"Earlier, when I went home," Kayla said, feeling everybody's attention in the room on her. "My little brother and sister was out front, playing in the snow."

"Yeah, yeah," Lorna said.

"And when they came inside, they told me that some guys in a car pulled up and asked if Marcus was there," Kayla said.

Lorna's eyes widened. Her head began to shake as she covered her mouth and looked at her son. Marcus, too, looked surprised. Immediately, he wanted to know why Kayla was waiting to just now say something. Before he could even open his mouth to say something, Kayla picked up on what was coming and got ahead of it.

"I don't know why I didn't say nothin'," Kayla said. "At first, I thought I was just bein' paranoid. I was gon' wait till later to maybe say somethin' but I been over here thinkin' bout it over and over. I know it couldn't have been Brandon and Juan cause when I got back up to the hospital earlier, y'all had said that they hadn't gone anyway."

Marcus shook his head. "Naw, they didn't," he said. "Not while you was gone, anyway. But what these two dudes look like?"

Kayla shrugged. "I don't know," she answered. "Latrell and Linell came back inside and told me that it was just two dudes that asked if you was there. I ain't get to see'em or nothing."

"You be over in her area providing your services?" Lorna asked her son, emphasizing the word "services."

Marcus, reluctantly, answered. "I mean," he said. "I know a couple niggas over there, but not like that."

"All it takes is one," Roy said. "I don't wanna tell you to not worry, cause I know I would be worrying a little bit, but it could just be a coincidence. If he deal with people over there then they might think that he stay over there. Just make sure when you go home and shit tonight, to watch your back. Make sure you constantly looking at your surroundings."

Kayla nodded. "I will," she said, in understanding.

Just then, a nurse came into the room. She announced that she was there to get the process started for Marcus going home tonight instead of staying the night in the hospital. Even to her, the tension in the room was high as everyone dispersed from the end of the bed when she entered. As Roy stepped to the side, he looked at his nephew – a cold, long look in the eye. This right here let Marcus know exactly what he was thinking.

***

Terrell sat across from Brandon and Juan, smoking on his cigarette, in the front room of his house on King. He had just told Brandon and Juan about what Marcus was caught up in. He was now taking in their surprised face, letting him know that they clearly had no idea.

"Marcus was fuckin' round with Tweety?" Brandon asked, surprised.

Terrell nodded. "Yup," he said. "Or, at least, that's what they out there sayin'. Word got around fast that he smashed her too. Hakim hit me up when he heard about it since I know Marcus more-so than he do."

Just then, Brandon and Juan made eye contact – the kind of eye contact that friends make when they know just what the other one is thinking. At that very moment, they both were wondering why Terrell hadn't hit up Marcus about all of this. Brandon then thought about why Marcus had not told either him or Juan about this.

"Man, I don' t know," Brandon said. "I don't know if I believe that."

"Yeah," Juan said, shaking his head. "I mean, why would Marcus smash Hakim's girl like that when he got his own, Kayla?"

Terrell looked at Juan and Brandon as if that was a stupid question. "Nigga, what you mean," he said. "You seen Tweety, haven't you?"

Brandon and Juan nodded before Juan answered. "Fuck yeah," he said. "She bad."

"Bad ain't even the word, my nigga," Terrell said. "That bitch got a ass that won't quit. I know y'all heard about the last nigga that fucked around with Hakim's chick."

"Naw," Brandon said, shaking his head. "I mean, before you, we ain't really know him like that. We had heard of him and met him around at a couple places, but never really talked to him or no shit like that."

"Well," Terrell said. "Let's just say it ain't turn out good for that nigga. From what I heard, Hakim embarrassed that nigga on his own fuckin' street. Held a gun to his head, made him strip down to where he was naked." Terrell's head shook. "After he talked shit to him right there in front of everybody, while he was naked, he told the nigga to walk his lil' dick self home. Apparently, when he got down the street a little ways, Hakim started firing his gun, making him cut out running, naked like that, between two houses and shit. He ain't never show his face on his own street again."

"Damn," Brandon said, shaking his head. "That shit is foul."

"Right," Terrell said, nodding. "Just imagine if you combine fuckin' around with his chick with some of his shit coming up missing from the trip up from down south. Ya boy Marcus is out here in a lot of trouble."

"And he ain't even tell us," Brandon said, trying to make sense of all this.

"Well," Terrell said. "When Hakim called me to ask me if I knew anything about it, I kept it one hundred with him. I told him I really ain't know the nigga like that, and I damn sure ain't know that he was smashin' his chick. If I knew he was gon' do some shit like that, I put that on everything I would have warned him and shit, just like I warned you. You don't wanna fuck around with no nigga's woman if you can help it. You sure don't wanna fuck around with Hakim's, let alone fuck with his shit."

There was then a long, awkward silence.

"So, now Hakim sayin' that Marcus done smashed his chick, Tweety?" Juan asked.

"Yep," Terrell answered. "I ain't know y'all even knew Tweety."

"I used to stay over by her when I lived out east," Brandon said. "So, that's how I know her. I feel like she mighta been in a couple of classes with my half-sister back in high school and maybe I used to hear about her that way too. I seen her, though. She bad."

"Yeah, you right about that," Juan said. "I only knew her by her name but I never had really had much interaction or nothin' with her."

"Hold up, though," Brandon said. "How do Marcus even know her like that, to where he would be smashing her and shit?"

"That's what I thought you would know," Terrell said. "And more importantly, where did it go down and how did Hakim find out about it? It's interesting he found out about that after Marcus come back with that work from down south and the shit come up short."

"Maybe he did smash that Tweety chick," Brandon said. "But I don't know if I believe that he would drive all the way back up from Texas or Arkansas or Louisiana or wherever and short that nigga Hakim on his own shit. I mean, Marcus ain't no dummy. He know that just like him, everybody else got scales and stuff too to know how much of what is going where. That is the part that just don't make no sense to me, nigga. I'm havin' a hard time believin' that."

"I was thinkin' the same thing," Terrell said, putting his cigarette out into a plant by the window behind where he sat. "But I know that that's the shit that got Hakim fired up. He sounded super shitty when he called me. Now that I think about it, he was also sayin' some shit about how he had talked to ya boy Marcus about everything and how he just didn't like bein' lied to and shit."

Juan and Brandon made eye contact with one another again.

"Look, niggas," Terrell said, standing back up. He could feel his dick was getting to the point where he was ready to get back into his bedroom and finish what he was doing with the thick redbone. "I got this phat ass hoe in there right now waitin' on this dick," Terrell said. "So I'mma just keep it one hundred with the two of you since y'all niggas seem like cool dudes and stuff. I know Marcus is your boy and shit and you just lookin' out for him, like any real niggas would. But, take it from me or not, you might wanna fall back a little bit until all this blow over. That nigga Hakim is fuckin' fired up about whatever went wrong between him and Marcus. And I don't think he the kinda nigga who just gon let it go and forget about it. Somethin' tellin' me that once he find out that Marcus is in the hospital and didn't get killed, there gon be some more sparks. Might be best if y'all just stay out the way and lay low before somebody come lookin' for one of you cause they think you got somethin' to do with it."

On that note, Brandon and Juan stood up. They shook hands with Terrell, as it was clear that he was about to go on back to handling his business. As Terrell saw them out, he told them to be careful out there. Brandon and Juan walked down the walkway from Terrell's front door to Brandon's Chevy Impala. As soon as they got into their seats, they looked at each other. Everything seemed to get so real at that very moment.

"So," Juan said. "What you wanna do?"

Letting his car warm up a little bit, Brandon leaned his head back into the headrest and thought about it for a second. He sure was not expecting to hear the things they'd heard from Terrell – things that would change the entire situation. Hakim was what can only be described as well established. If he indeed was after Marcus, he would be a lot harder to deal with than some ordinary nigga out in the street. And Brandon and Juan both knew that.

***

Back at the hospital, in Marcus' room, the nurse held a clipboard and went over some things with Marcus. As he already knew, he would have to come back in to see the doctor. Physical rehabilitation was required whether he liked it or not. All the while the nurse got Marcus' paperwork together, there was a noticeable tension in the room. Roy, Kayla, and Lorna simply sat over on the other side of the room while Marcus answered the questions.

Much confusion was brewing at the back of Marcus' mind. He knew that Kayla still had his phone, somewhere. Asking for it would definitely set off a red flag of sorts. Rather, he knew he would just have to wait until he was officially released before he hit his boys up. He wanted to know what they had found out – if they had found out that the two dudes who shot up his apartment were sent by Hakim. He knew that if this was the case – and it probably was – he'd probably have a little explaining to do. Nonetheless, he continued to weigh his options. As soon as the nurse walked out of the room to go put the information from the paperwork into the computer, Lorna stood up and came straight for the edge of the bed.

"Tonight," she said. "What we gon' do is take you back to my place, Marcus. Then, once you've slept a little bit, we can get workin' on getting you up to Fort Wayne as soon as possible. Ain't no point in you even thinkin' that you gon' just be walkin' round Indianapolis like ain't nothin' happen. Last thing you need if for somebody to come for you out in some parking lot or something and all you got is a fuckin' cast on and your arm in a sling. We not even gon do that shit."

"What about my appointment's, Mama?" Marcus asked, looking away from his mother. Her overbearing ways could really push him to his limits, but he kept is cool. "You heard the doctor? I'mma have to come back for visits and then the physical therapy."

"Nigga, they got that shit up in Fort Wayne," Lorna said. "Ain't like Fort Wayne is no little town or nothing, Marcus. They got all this same shit up there. And it would probably be even better if you do it up there."

"Why you say it'd be better if I do it up there?" Marcus asked.

Just then, Lorna slanted her eyes at a nurse walking back. She was black with long blonde hair extensions and very easily could have been from the hood.

"You don't always know who's takin' care of you," Lorna said. "For all you know, whoever work here, could know whoever the hell this is that shot up your place. At least in Fort Wayne, you ain't gotta worry about knowin' nobody. The only person you know up there is your cousin Larry. But, I will tell you this, though."

"What?" Marcus asked.

"Don't go gettin' involved in this same kinda shit up there," Lorna warned. "You need to be up there gettin' your arm back together and sittin' in the house, minding your damn business. Maybe you should take this as a warning sign, Marcus. As much as you don't want to, maybe you should take this as a sign from God that it's time for you to do something different with your life – something to where you ain't gotta worry about people coming after you and shit."

"Mama, whatever," Marcus said, looking away.

Ever since Marcus was a teenager, he had found that he had far more success making his money in the streets. He worked at a McDonald's that was downtown inside of a hotel when he was fifteen years old. After five or six months of that – something which he compared to slave labor once he saw his paycheck – he definitely knew that working in the fast food or restaurant industry was not going to work for him. He was playing basketball when he was in high school, but got to the point where he was too busy making money to show up for practices. Plus, after a while, he started to see high schools just exploit players to make money and build a name for themselves. When he would hear some of the school profits on the news and whatnot and think about how he was being paid absolutely nothing to play on the school's team, he decided that he was out. Any dream of every making the NBA was too far – and too unlikely – away. When he graduated from high school, he was making enough money in the street that he really didn't need a job. However, when an old buddy of his got on at UPS, making good money with benefits, Marcus had decided to go ahead and give that a try. He worked there for three weeks – three long weeks – before the administration had found that it made a mistake in processing is information. Human Resources had failed to direct Marcus to taking his pre-employment drug screening. When Marcus went and took the test, he found out some days later that he failed and was terminated from working there. That was okay, though. He didn't really care for throwing around a bunch of boxes anyway. The very thought of him going out into the racist world and trying to please the white man to get a job just did not sit well with him.

All the while Lorna had been telling Marcus her ideal plan for keeping his low until things blew over, Kayla could not help but to stare at Marcus. In the back of her mind, she replayed the scene from earlier – the scene where she was in the bathroom when the shots began. This, of course, would only lead her to remembering how she'd found Marcus' on the floor in front of the glass patio door, shot. Still, though, Kayla could not wait to be alone with him after this long, hard, and scary day. She wanted him to tell her the truth, in all details, about why whoever could possibly be after him.

Within an hour's time, Marcus was allowed to get dressed. He was then escorted to another part of the hospital floor where nurses put his bandaged his arm up then put it into a sling.

"I ain't never had to wear one of these before," Marcus said, looking at Kayla and shaking his head. Lorna and Roy had stayed back in the waiting area by his room while Kayla walked with him and the nurse to get his arm bandaged up.

"Yeah," Kayla said, forcing a smile. "Just be glad that it ain't turn out worse, yet."

Marcus picked up on how Kayla had said the word 'yet.' Just as he was about to speak, the nurse came back over to finish up with Marcus' arm. When she finished, Marcus and Kayla told her thank you and headed back down the hall, toward the waiting area by his room.

"You scared, ain't you baby?" Marcus came out and asked.

Kayla, who was walking at Marcus' side and being extra careful that he not bump his arm into anything, looked at him. She could not help but to think about the car that had asked if he was at her house.

"I mean," she said, hesitantly. "A little bit. I mean, do you really sell over in my neighborhood to where they would know, or think, that you might be there sometimes?"

Marcus nodded slightly. "Yeah," he said. "I got some niggas over there I fuck with. And it ain't no secret me and you together."

"So," Kayla said. "When you gon' tell me who it is that might have done this? You think they gon' come back?"

"I'mma ride with you," Marcus said. "You can take me back to my place to get a few things then over to my mama house, if you ain't gotta go home and help with your brother and sister."

Kayla shook her head. "Naw," she said. "My mama is just gon' actually have to be a mother tonight until I get home. I know she gon' be mad, but I don't care."

"You know how she is," Marcus said then snickered.

"Yeah," Kayla said, rolling her eyes. "She been blowin' my phone up... Prolly had some man that was try'na get with her and so she was try'na hurry up and get over to wherever he is. She'll be okay without all that tonight."

"You know she gon' be on your shit about all of this, don't you?" Marcus said.

"I know, I know," Kayla said. "She already said what she had to say earlier. So, Marcus, I wanna know, though, is there anything that you keepin' from me? Could these people be rolling by my house cause they think you might be there?"

"I'mma tell you everything in the car," Marcus promised. "And no, I can't think of any reason why they would even be after you. It's some straight bullshit that they even after me. I told them I did not do this, but, as you can see, they don't wanna go for it."

"Do you think your mother is right?" Kayla asked, softly.

"About what?" Marcus asked.

"Brandon and Juan," she said. "You think there is any way that they coulda had something to do with any of this."

Without a second thought, Marcus began to shake his head. "Hell naw," he said. "Don't go buyin' into my mama shit. That's all she want people to do is to believe her and everything that she got to say. I put that on everything I own that there ain't no way that Brandon and Juan got anything to do with any of this. I can just about guarantee you that they out looking for whoever did this shit right now. Shit, or at least they try'na see if they can find out. That's the part I don't like."

"The part you don't like?" Kayla asked. Just as she was about to add on more to her question, she and Marcus were coming to the waiting area. Roy and Lorna, who had been talking back and forth to one another, stood up. Kayla smiled, knowing that she was going to have a real talk with Marcus as soon as they got into her car.

"I'mma take him back to his place to get some things then I'mma bring him over to your place," Kayla said to Miss Lorna.

Lorna grinned. "Okay," she said. "Just be careful, please. Watch everything and everyone around you in case these fools just so happen to show back up over there. Get in and get out and hurry up and get only what you need."

"Marcus," Roy said, in a very commanding way. "I'mma hit you up tomorrow to see how you doin."

Marcus nodded at his uncle, knowing exactly what that meant. He could tell that his uncle was trying his hardest to keep his composure. It would not surprise Marcus one bit if his Uncle Roy already had his ears and eyes out in the hood, trying to get to the bottom of this. Marcus immediately got nervous at just the thought of that. The deal he had made with Hakim was completely and totally separate from anything having to do with his Uncle Roy. And Marcus knew that his Uncle Roy was not going to like hearing something like that. Roy had always taught Marcus that the best way to stay safe out in these streets, if staying safe was something that was even possible, was to keep it all in the family. The very fact that Marcus's place had been shot up at all told Roy that his nephew must not have been doing that. Marcus knew that Roy was not going to bring it up in front of his girlfriend and mother. However, he could tell by the look in his eyes that he had a lot of unanswered questions – questions that there would definitely be no escaping now.

Lorna and Roy just so happened to be parked on the opposite side of the hospital from where Kayla had parked her car. They all rode the elevator downstairs together, splitting up on the ground floor. Now it was just Marcus and Kayla, finally to themselves after this crazy day, as they walked to the parking garage. Curse words immediately slipped out of Marcus' mouth as soon as the double doors to the parking garage opened and the cold, winter wind came rushing in. He had been wearing his sweatpants and a sweater the hospital staff found for him to put on. As he got into the passenger side seat of Kayla's car, Marcus struggled a bit with putting on his seatbelt. Once he got it on, he relaxed and pushed his head back into the headrest. It was now going on 11 o'clock at night. He'd only been in the hospital for eight or nine hours and already missed the feeling of something as simple as a seat in a car.

Kayla backed out of her parking spot and started making her way toward the parking garage cashier.

"I know I'mma sleep good tonight," Marcus said, in a very positive way.

Soon enough, they had paid at the parking garage and we on the highway, headed out east on Interstate 70.

"So, Marcus," Kayla said, letting him that she wanted some explanation. "What the fuck is all this about?"

Marcus took a deep breath, really wishing that none of this had happened and that he did not have to tell his chick.

"Okay," Marcus said. "Remember when I took that trip down south to get that work."

"Yeah," Kayla said, nodding. "For the Makim dude?"

"Yeah," Marcus said. "And his name is Hakim, not Makim. Well, yeah, so the nigga had me drive down there to get the shit from his connect, I guess after it come across the border or something." Marcus knew that he had to watch his words very carefully, as he did not want to tell Kayla everything. "Well, I get the shit back up here, on the day I'm supposed to, and the nigga ain't at his place. Come to find out, he had to go outta town for some family emergency or something. I think he went to Cincinnati or Dayton or some shit in Ohio. So, I hit him up and tell him at his fuckin' place with his shit. He tell me sorry this and sorry that, that he wasn't there to meet me. He told me that his garage was open and that I could pull inside of there and use his tools and shit to get the bricks out of the paneling in the car."

"Okay, okay," Kayla said. "So what's the problem, Marcus? Why would he be after you and try'na shoot your place up and shit?"

"Cause," Marcus said. "Dude ain't come back for like a week and that trip was like what, two or three weeks ago. Well, a couple weeks ago he come callin' me sayin' some shit about how one of the bricks wasn't right. He said some shit about how there was like a hole in one of them and the weight was off or something. I don't know. I just told the nigga, like dude, I ain't got your shit. I did the part I was supposed to do. Long story short, we got into on the phone, with him throwing around a bunch of numbers and shit about whatever was missing and how much it all come up to be. I told him check with his niggas in Dallas about all that. Why would I steal however much of his cocaine? I went out and looked in the panels of the car and everything. No white shit nowhere. I called him and told the nigga, I ain't got your shit."

"But he convinced that you do?" Kayla asked, just for clarification.

Marcus looked across at Kayla, knowing that he had left a big part of the story out. "Yeah," he said, basically.

At the back of Marcus' mind, he could not help but to think about the gap in the story. He could have sworn on his own life that he would never fuck around on Kayla when they first met and things started to get serious between the two of them. However, when he lay eyes on Tweety, that all changed. Tweety was the one who had been at Hakim's house when he got there after the trip down south. At first, knowing the kind of nigga that Hakim is, Marcus played it cool and kept it respectful. However, even he could not deny how Tweety was practically throwing it at him. And it was all for his taking.

Tweety could only be described as a bad bitch. She was all tens, from the face all the way down to her feet. With a nice brown complexion, her skin was smooth and flawless. She was wearing just enough makeup to accentuate her pretty face, but not so much that it would take away from it. Her ass was the kind of ass that many chicks nowadays would pay for or be in the gym eight days a week, doing squats to get – the kind of ass that Marcus could see from the front. One thing led to another and she was on her knees, sucking his dick just inside Hakim's front room. Marcus knew that it was wrong, and even more so wrong because of who she belonged to. However, after feeling her silky mouth slide all the way down his shaft, almost effortlessly, the last thing on his mind was some nigga who was out of town. Next thing next, she was bent over the couch with Marcus hitting it from the back. And she was a squirter at that, which only pushed Marcus over the edge even further.

Marcus looked at Kayla, knowing that he needed to say something to get her to calm down just a little bit.

"Kayla," Marcus said. "You know a nigga is gon' handle this shit."

"How?" Kayla asked, clearly irritated and with thoughts swirling around in her mind. "Tomorrow or the day after, you gon' be headed up to Fort Wayne, Marcus. What does that mean for me, huh? Huh? I'mma be the one left down here with these people may be coming after me."

"Shit," Marcus said. "I think you just bein' paranoid, Kayla. Like my uncle said, all that could have just been a coincidence that whoever was rolling by your place and asking for me. If they really thought I was there, do you really think that they would have been asking if I was there? They sure ain't ask when they came to my place. They just showed up and started shooting."

"This is different, though, Marcus," Kayla said. "I got my little brother and sister and stuff."

"I know, I know," Marcus said. "But I promise you, baby, I think you just overreacting. Plus, I put it on my life, I ain't tell Hakim no shit about you or where you live."

"So," Kayla said. "You know how this city is. Just cause you ain't tell him don't mean that he ain't find out from somebody or something. It ain't like people in that life don't know we together and shit, and plus I been living where I stay a lot longer than you been living over off Shadeland, you know? How do you even know this Hakim nigga, anyway, Marcus? Huh? How the fuck you even know him? Is it somebody that your uncle set you up with?"

Marcus shook his head. "Hell naw," he answered. "You know how my uncle feel about this shit. He think you should only work with family if you wanna stay safe."

"Yeah, I could tell at the hospital that he was kinda shitty about something, but I ain't know what," Kayla said.

"Yeah, well," Marcus said, looking out over the east side as the highway inclined above the roofs of houses. "I already know he prolly gon' get in my shit tomorrow."

Kayla sniffled. Just then thought of Marcus going up to Ft. Wayne to lay kind of made her sad.

"So," Kayla said. "You really gon' lay low up in Fort Wayne like your mama said?"

Marcus looked away, still not being all that keen on the idea. "I mean..." he said. "I guess I'mma have to. Do I want to? Fuck no? I ain't scared of these niggas. How's it gon' look if I'm bein' ran up out my own city like this?"

"But you was sure lookin' out the patio door earlier today," Kayla said. "I noticed you doin' that, so don't even say that you wasn't."

Marcus knew that he might as well go ahead and be honest about that part. "Yeah," he said. "I was. I ain't gon' front. That Hakim nigga had said he was gon' hear from me, but I ain't know what he meant."

"And it ain't even fuckin' occur to you to fuckin' tell me, Marcus?" Kayla asked, starting to feel deep into her feelings. "What if they woulda shot me or some shit, huh? You think about that? What if one of them bullets would have got me or something?"

This part of the possible scenarios was one that really got to Marcus. Deep down, he felt guilty that he did not tell the woman he loved about Hakim's round-about threat. He felt so stupid looking back at it now. However, not telling Kayla seemed to be the right thing to do at the time. He didn't want her to get all worked up over something that might not even be legit. Furthermore, Marcus was even trying to go over and talk to Hakim about it all, to let him know that he really did not take the half a brick. He honestly did not know how a hole got into the side of the brick. And he wondered where so much could have spilled out without him even noticing.

Marcus also knew that the cherry on top of the shit he was caught up in was the fact that he smashed Hakim's chick. This was not the first time that he'd gotten a dude super mad about taking down his chick probably better than he could. However, this dude was different – this dude was one that Marcus knew he should not have messed with in any way at all. He felt so guilty about it all looking back. However, in the moment also, it felt so good. She had that pussy that he could only describe as far. At the same time, Marcus could not think of any reason that Tweety would tell Hakim about what happened between the two of them – not unless she was the kind of chick to play games. Marcus had already learned in life the way some women will try to use another man to make their own man jealous. At this point, he could only hope that that was not Tweety's game. Aside from talking to Hakim, Marcus wished that he could find a way to talk to Tweety. If anybody would have some information that he could use right now, it would be her. Nonetheless, he did not have her phone number and had failed to find her when he searched on Facebook.

Kayla drove the rest of the way to the Shadeland Avenue exit on Interstate 70 without saying much of anything.

Suddenly, her world had changed and was going to continuing to change. As soon as tomorrow, Marcus would be headed up to Ft. Wayne to stay low while she had to look over her shoulder to make sure that Hakim and his boys were not shooting up her house. Yes, she believed that Marcus probably had not told Hakim and whoever else where his girlfriend lived. However, at the same time, she knew that Indianapolis was only so big, and it was small when you're black. People talked and talked and talked as if it was a small town and not a city of a million people.

"I don't know, Marcus," Kayla said. "I just don't know. This shit is kinda scary."

"We gon' be alright, baby," Marcus said. "We gon' be alright. Like we sat at the hospital, I'mma go chill with my cousin Larry up in Fort Wayne for a little while...until Hakim move on with this fuckin' shit and realize that I ain't got his stuff."

"And what if he don't, Marcus?" Kayla asked. "What if he ain't the kinda nigga to let go of the situation and move on? What if he one of them niggas who gon' be lookin' for your ass for years or some shit?"

That is exactly what Marcus was scared of. He knew that part of Hakim's furiousness with him had to have something to do with his chick Tweety. At the same time, he practically racked his mind until he was tired trying to figure out who would have even told Hakim that he smashed his chick down in the living room that day when he got back from down south. In fact, Marcus still had the text message in his phone from Hakim – a text message that said Hakim had sent, saying that he was going to fuck Marcus up for "getting into what was his."

Marcus kept an eye out for any and everything when Kayla pulled into the parking lot of his apartment complex and around to his building. Everything seemed so calm – seemed as if a dozen or so bullets had not been flying just earlier that day. Nonetheless, that still didn't mean that whoever Hakim had sent would not be coming back around to see if Marcus came back. Marcus knew this and this is why he was already making a little list in his mind of the stuff he would hurry and get.

Kayla pulled into a parking spot a few spots down from where she would normally park. Even in the dark of the winter night, she and Marcus could see how the landlord had to board up Marcus' apartment. The door to his apartment from the outside, rather, was still intact and simply shut. Kayla handed Marcus her keys since they had not remembered to get his before he left. She then grabbed his cell phone out of the side compartment of her car door and handed it to him.

"You want me to come in with you and help?" Kayla asked.

Marcus shook his head, feeling the stiffness in his shoulder get stronger and stronger as the "juice," as he called it, started to wear off. "Naw, baby," he said. "Just sit out here and chill for a second. I'mma only be a minute."

"Okay," Kayla said. "If I see anything, I'mma call you. Just please, Marcus, don't turn on no lights. Let's make this quick so don't no more shit pop off or nothin'."

"Aight," Marcus said, as he opened his car door. "I'll be right back."

Marcus virtually disappeared, using the light in his cell phone to guide his way as he looked around his apartment. He got some change of clothes, a couple pairs of shoes, and grabbed some money he had stashed away.

Kayla had never felt so nervous in her life. Part of her felt like she might feel safer with this entire situation if the hospital had just kept Marcus in overnight. Every so often, she would glance at the time on her car stereo and realize that tomorrow would come faster than she knew it. It was so crazy how just practically twelve hours before this point she had been lying in bed with Marcus on a snowy day, to say the least. It was so crazy how quickly things changed.

As Kayla was thinking about everything that had happened, headlights slowly turned in from the main road of the apartment complex that led out to Shadeland Avenue. Kayla noticed immediately how the car was moving rather slowly, especially considering how the sunny part of the day had virtually melted all the snow and ice on the surface of the parking lot. Quickly, without even thinking, she grabbed her phone and called inside to Marcus. He answered.

"Watch out," Kayla said. "This car movin' real slow in the parking lot and I don't know what they bout to do." Kayla dipped down in her seat, moving her head ever so slightly to watch where the car went.

Inside, Marcus ducked down. He also watched where he stood, being sure to not stand in any light that was shining inside from the windows that were not shattered during the shooting. From where he stood, in the living room, he could see out to the parking lot and see the very same car that Kayla was talking about. "Yeah, I see it," he said.

Soon enough, the car came to a stop. Three small children began to climb out of the backseat then an adult out of the front passenger side seat. Instantly, both Marcus and Kayla both relaxed.

"I'mma hurry up and come out, okay," Marcus said then hung up.

Marcus quickly grabbed the rest of the things he had come to get and was heading back out to the car. Kayla quickly pulled out of the parking spot and headed over to Marcus' mother's house. Lorna lived in a cute little ranch style house, not too far from where Marcus lived. She had lived in it for a few years, but had put enough work into the yard to where you would have thought she lived there for decades. Even covered in snow, anyone could see the outline of the flowerbeds and the brick-lined walkway.

Kayla pulled the car up out front. They could already see that Lorna was home because there were a few lights on in the house. Marcus began to take his seatbelt off and push his car door open. He noticed that Kayla was not moving, or at least as quickly as he was. He stopped and looked over at her.

"Baby," Marcus said. "Ain't you gon' come in?"

Kayla shook her head. "Naw," she said. "I mean, I want to, but I prolly need to go home to my brother and sister. Make sure my mama ain't left them at home alone or some dumb shit. You know how she is, Marcus."

"Is that what you over there thinking about, Kayla?" Marcus asked. There was clearly a bit of disgruntled feelings in his tone. "Huh?"

Kayla looked over at Marcus and could see that he was somewhat upset, judging by the way his forehead was wrinkled up.

"Ain't no need to catch no attitude with me," Kayla let him know. "Let's not forget that I'm the one who almost got my head blown off today cause you done got caught up in some shit with that nigga, whatever his name is."

"I know, I know," Marcus said. "And I'm fuckin' sorry. Trust me, girl. I love you. I would never wanna put you in no kind of harm's way. You think I ain't been thinkin' bout this shit just like you have? Of course I have. I mean, I almost lost my fuckin' life today and all over some shit that I ain't even do."

"Yeah, well, you not about to lose me," Kayla said.

"What the fuck you mean I ain't about to lose you?" Marcus asked.

Kayla looked at him, dead in the eyes. "You the one who gon be going out of town to lay low tomorrow. Where does that put me? You think about that? What if that was them coming by my house, asking for you? I really don't think it was just some coincidence that they just so happy to come by on the very same day that you got shot and sitting up in the hospital. Yeah, I could be wrong. And I certainly hope that I am wrong, but still. Plus, what if this shit don't just roll over like you all think it will?"

"So, what?" Marcus asked. "What? You thinkin' that this dude is gon' come traveling all over the world to find me or some shit, huh? Huh?"

"I don't fuckin' know," Kayla said. "You the one who supposedly know the nigga…I don't. You tell me. If he was angry enough to shoot up your place like that, who is to say that he might not try some other kind of way to get you whenever he fuckin' feel like it. He clearly pretty fuckin' shitty. Plus, unless I heard you wrong, you said you saw the two dudes from when you was standing in your patio doorway. You ain't saying that you saw this nigga who you supposedly in some deep shit with."

"Yeah?" Marcus said, wondering where she was going.

"Yeah, so..." Kayla said. "That tell me that this nigga must have a little money to be payin' people to do some shit like this, or at least some niggas he cool with that got the time to be doin it."

"Look, why don't you go to Fort Wayne with me, then?" Marcus asked. "What you got here in Indianapolis? Nothin. You young and try'na be a mother to them kids, Kayla. Them not your kids. You don't gotta do what you doin' for them you know. Maybe if you stopped doin' that shit, then their real mother would actually step up and do it. Fuck, she ain't gon do it if she know that if she don't do it, then you will just step in and do it."

"Get out," Kayla said. "Get the fuck outta my car right now."

"And now you mad at me and shit?" Marcus asked. "Look, Kayla, I ain't no happier than you are about this shit. I swear to God I ain't. But you actin' like this ain't gon do shit to make it no better. I'm just try'na offer you a different option. That's why I said we should move to Atlanta. You and me and nobody fuckin' else has to know."

"You was sayin' that shit because you knew your ass was caught up in some shit and you wanted to get out of town before the shit started to look bad for you, Marcus," Kayla said. "That's why your ass was try'na move to Atlanta and don't even act like it wasn't."

"Kayla," Marcus said, now getting a little angry. "I told you that I had been thinkin' bout that shit and I really had been. Why you try'na act like this and you know that I might be goin' outta town tomorrow and layin' low for a little bit? You realize what the fuck be on my mind right now. I got the fuckin' police breathin' all down my neck and shit. You know how they love to lock niggas up over any damn things. Yeah, sure, they might not do much investigating over this. But what happens if something else pops up and they try'na get me cause I look suspicious to them or something? Aside from that, I gotta worry about some niggas being after me and try'na shoot my fuckin' head off. I ain't even gon have two arms for a minute."

"Okay, so why not just stop then Marcus?" Kayla asked, in a very serious and calm tone.

"Why not just stop what?" Marcus asked, confused.

"Stop this shit out in these streets," Kayla said. "Why don't you just stop that shit and, like your mama said, take what happened earlier today as a big wakeup call? Just stop before the shit get even worse."

"So now you want me to stop this shit, huh?" Marcus said. "You for real? You want me to stop now, do you? You sure wasn't sayin' that shit when I was taken you out to them nice restaurants. What about all them clothes I bought you, huh? Kayla? I bet you that you still got that shit and still wear that shit any fuckin' chance you get. You ain't say all that when I was payin' to get your hair done, buying you any kind of jewelry you wanted at the mall."

At that moment, for the first time during their relationship, Kayla felt vulnerable and a little guilty. She was well aware that so many of the nice things that she had she would not have had if it were not for Marcus. In so many ways, he spoiled her and made her feel so pretty. Now, however, she was starting to see the downside to that kind of lifestyle. It was as if she always knew that that downside existed; she just did not think that it would hit so close to home, so fast. Seeing Marcus lying on the floor, shot in the shoulder after bullets practically sprayed into the apartment, made her think of everything in a different light. All of the sudden, all of those nice things that he'd gotten for her meant absolutely nothing at all.

"I'd rather have you," Kayla came out and said. "Marcus, I'd rather have you than to have all that shit. That shit don't mean shit to me if I ain't got you. I guess that's what I'm try'na get you to see." Kayla's eyes swelled up with tears. She didn't normally think of herself as the emotional kind of chick, but when she got into her feelings, that side could definitely come out of her.

Hearing this point of view from his mother was nothing new for Marcus. However, hearing the same thing from his girl's point of view really made him look at it differently. Marcus pulled the door back closed and pushed his head into the head rest of his seat.

"Marcus, this shit ain't even worth it if you ask me," Kayla said. "You ain't makin' enough money that it's worth your life."

"I told you, though, Kayla," Marcus said. "I ain't even do it. Whatever they put in the car before I left Dallas is what I took to his house. I put it right where he told me to put it, cause his ass wasn't even there. Look, baby, I know you scared and stuff but you can't go thinking like that now."

"Thinking like what?" Kayla asked. "A rational chick."

Marcus pushed his car door open. Immediately, cold air whipped inside of the car. Kayla turned and looked the other way, feeling a cold tear start to stroll down the side of her face. Quickly, she wiped it away.

"I'll text you later on if you wanna talk or anything," Marcus said. "I really am sorry about today, Kayla. I am. I never meant for none of this shit to effect you like this."

Kayla sniffled. "I know," she said, nodding her head. "I know."

On that note, Marcus pushed Kayla's car door closed and headed up the driveway, into her mother's house. He was leaving one stress behind (Kayla and what she was talking about) to go deal with another (his overbearing mother).

Chapter 3

Kayla decided to take the street way home instead of the interstate. Since the streets were practically clear, especially toward the middle lanes, she knew that she could just take her sweet time – sit in her thoughts and really reflect on the entire day. There was no doubt that there would probably be some form of mothering when she got home that she would have to do.

Just as Kayla pulled up to a stoplight near Miss Lorna's house, she could feel her phone vibrating in her pocket. She sighed as she rolled her eyes and pulled her phone out of her pocket. To her relief, it was not her mother calling. Rather, it was her girl, Myesha.

"Hello?" Kayla answered.

"Whew, girl," Myesha said. "Please do not take this the wrong way, but you definitely do not sound too good right now."

"Girl, I'm fine," Kayla said. "I just got into it with Marcus when I was droppin' him off at his mama house. I don't know if I told you earlier or not, but the doctor said that he could leave the hospital tonight instead of having to spend the night and stuff. They got him all bandaged up with his arm in a sling."

"Well, that's good," Myesha said, trying to say sounding positive. "Girl, I was just hitting you up to see how you were doing. I remember earlier how you were all stressed out and stuff."

"Girl, that wasn't even the end of it and now I really don't know what to think," Kayla said

"What, Kayla?" Myesha asked. "What you mean that wasn't the end of it? Girl, what done happened now?"

Kayla shook her head. "Myesha, girl, I been up at the hospital all night," she said. "And you not gon' believe what's gon be happening tomorrow?"

"What?" Myesha asked, clearly very interested.

"Marcus is gon be going up north," Kayla said. "He gon' lay low up there until all of this blow over, or so they hope."

"Up north?" Myesha asked. "When, and how, did they decide that he would be going up to north? Where he gon' be goin' up north?"

"His mama," Kayla said. "They got a cousin up there that she talked to who said that he could come stay up there. Girl, this nigga done got somebody after him."

"Are you serious?" Myesha asked. "Who?"

"Girl, I don't even know myself," Kayla said, lying. She knew right away that she was not going to tell even her best friend Myesha everything about what was going on. Knowledge is power and she did not want to give anyone else any more power of her than they already had. It was safe so say that her nerves were already on edge. The last thing in the world she needed was for somebody to know too much. "Some nigga that him and his boys, I guess, did a bad deal with or something. Now, from the sounds of it, this dude, who name I can't even remember, is going after Marcus. Marcus swore up and down to me that he ain't even do it, but I just don't know what to believe right now."

"Where is he even going up north?" Myesha asked. "Why?"

"I forget the name of the town," Kayla lied. "Somewhere up north, I think near the border with Michigan or something. Anyway, he got a cousin who live up there that his mama talked to today. Dude said that he could come stay with him until everything blows over, if everything blows over."

"How long is that going to be?" Myesha asked. "Are you thinking about what if whoever these people are come back after Marcus or something? What if they hear about where he is and come after him there?"

"Girl, I tried to bring all that up," Kayla said. "I really did and he seem to think that I'm being paranoid. We got into it real bad when I was droppin' him off at his mama house just now."

"Over what?" Myesha asked.

"Girl, he just don't get it," Kayla said, shaking her head while keeping her eyes on the road. "He seem to think that whoever did this is just gon' let it go. I told him, and so did his mama and his uncle, that when whoever find out that they bullet did not kill him, there was no doubt in my mind that they would try again. Whoever got fucked over in this deal, or thinks that he got fucked over, obviously must have some money if they sendin' niggas after you and shit. That's what I told Marcus. And if they ain't got no money, they damn sure got them some buddies who got time for this kinda bullshit. Girl, I am so tired."

"I bet you are" Myesha said. "So, he gon' be headed up there tomorrow?"

"That's the plan," Kayla said. "He gon' go up there tomorrow, I guess with his mama or uncle taking him, I don't know. It wasn't like I was even invited or nothing."

"Girl, you know you gon' ride up there with your boo," Myesha said and giggled. "I don't even know why you try'na act like you not. You gon' be right there in that car with him, Misses Ride or Die."

Kayla smiled. "Girl, shut up," she said. "You don't know that. So, what you doin?"

"Girl, just got back in the house," Myesha explained. "I went to meet up with my partner from class and get this book from her so I could use it. You remember, don't you? That girl I told you about that I was sharing a book with?"

Kayla thought about it for a second. "Yeah," she said. She then started to think about how right now she was talking to her best friend, who was in college and moving forward with her life. It was such a contrast to her own life, in her eyes, because here she was having to watch her back. At the back of her mind, she could not help but to fear the idea of whoever coming after Marcus coming after her. Sure, she thought about how she could indeed be overreacting. However, something deep down in Kayla's heart and soul told her that she was not.

"Girl," Kayla said, deciding that she might as well go ahead and tell Myesha about what happened with her brother and sister. "There's more, too. I'm so fuckin' nervous I swear I ain't never been so nervous in my life. I don't remember if I told you earlier, I don't think I did cause it was after we talked."

"What, girl?" Myesha said. "What?"

"Okay, so," Kayla started. "Earlier, when I got off the phone with you, I went downstairs, I called in Latrell and Linell from outside. They was out there playin' in the snow after they ate they little afternoon meal and stuff. So, yeah, I call them inside from the snow and stuff and you not gon' believe what they told me."

"What?" Myesha asked, practically on the edge of her seat even through the phone. "What, Kayla?"

"They told me that two dudes in a car rolled by while they was playing and stopped and asked if Marcus was there," Kayla said.

"No," Myesha said. "Are you serious? Girl, please be safe. Watch your back, I'm tell in you."

"Girl, I know," Kayla said. "At first I wasn't even gon' tell them, up at the hospital about it, but Miss Lorna, Marcus's mom, was really goin' in hard on Marcus's boys Brandon and Juan. And I really didn't think they did this and now I really don't because they was still at the hospital when I got back and Marcus and Lorna both said that they hadn't left."

"Well," Myesha said. "That's good you at least ex-ed them two off the list. But still, if somebody coming by your place asking for him then it really sound like he is involved in some deep shit. Girl, you sure that you shouldn't just go stay somewhere else too?"

"Girl, you know I can't do that," Kayla said. "I got Latrell and Linell. Their fuckin' lives would go to shambles if I left them with just Mama. I just can't do that right now, girl. I just can't."

"I feel you on that," Myesha said. "Your mama is really wilding out nowadays, ain't she?"

"Girl, yes," Kayla said. "She thinks she is like twenty-five or somethin' again, and it is really getting' ridiculous. You have no idea. My phone been blowin' up all day, basically since like a couple of hours after I left, and I know it's my mama calling. She probably wanted to know when I was comin' home so she could know when she could leave and lay up with some nigga. I'm on my way home now and, girl, I would not be the least bit surprised if I get there and she gone and done left my brother and sister to fend for themselves. I swear to God I'm gettin' so fuckin' tired of her I don't even know what to do. It's like sometimes she wants to be a mother while other times, it's like she's a teenage child with an attitude."

"Glad that ain't me," Myesha said, sounding relieved. "I don't know, though, girl. You might be surprised when you get home in a minute."

Kayla chuckled. "Why you say that?" she asked. "God knows I don't need no more fuckin' surprises right now. I had one big one that was several gunshots long this morning. That was enough for me."

"Yeah, I bet," Myesha said. "But no, that ain't what I'm talkin' bout. I'm talkin' bout she just might be there when you get home in a minute. When I rolled by your house earlier, when I was going to meet my classmate, there was this car parked out front that I'd never seen before. I figured it was either one of your neighbors, although I can't think of who, or some many that your mama had over. I remember how you told me that she be having men over in the middle of the night and stuff. I already knew that you'd be gone this afternoon and evening, so I figured she would just have them over instead of her going to wherever they stay."

"Fuck," Kayla said. "I hope she ain't got no nigga over there right now. That is some shit she would do, though. My boyfriend is up in the hospital, shot and shit, and she take it as her chance to have a date night with her two kids at home. How fuckin' trifling can you get? What the car look like when you seen it? Maybe I know which nigga it is tonight?"

"Girl, I ain't really look at it like that," Myesha said. "All I remember was that it was a black car. I don't know what kind of model, but I know I never seen it before."

"Wait a minute?" Kayla said, alarmed. "A black car? Parked out front of my house?"

"Yeah, girl," Myesha said. "Earlier, when I drove by, heading downtown to meet up with my classmate, I saw it. It was a black car, kinda shiny with some sort of rims on it. It just look like a nigga car, if you know what I mean."

"Oh shit, girl," Kayla said.

"What? What?" Myesha asked. "What's wrong, Kayla? What's wrong?"

Kayla's heart jumped. Suddenly, her hand holding the wheel felt very stiff; the several miles between where she was at the moment and where she lived seemed to be so far away.

"I fuckin' knew it!" Kayla yelled, almost forgetting that she was on the phone.

"Girl, what?" Myesha asked. "I'm confused. Girl, what are you talkin' about?"

"Earlier, when I found Marcus on the floor, he said that he saw a black car pull up and two niggas get out," Kayla said. "When Latrell and Linell were coming in from outside, they said that it was a black car. Girl, this shit ain't no coincidence. These the same people. They at my house."

At that moment, Kayla and Myesha could hear the other one breathing. All Kayla could think about was her brother and sister, and hope to God that this was just a third coincidence as she put the pedal to the metal.

BCPL
Baltimore County
Public Library

CPSIA information can be obtained
at www.ICGtesting.com
Printed in the USA
LVOW10s2008140617

538120LV00018B/395/P

9 781547 113064